HOLY Laughter

The Happy Hunters
Charles ♥ Frances

Published by
Hunter Books
201 McClellan Road
Kingwood, Texas 77339-2710
U.S.A.

Books By The Happy Hunters

A Confession A Day Keeps The Devil Away
Angels On Assignment
Are You Tired?
Born Again! What Do You Mean?
Come Alive
Follow Me
Go, Man, Go
God Is Fabulous
God's Answer To Fat...Loøse It!
God's Conditions For Prosperity
Handbook For Healing
Hang Loose With Jesus
Healing
Heart To Heart Flip Chart
His Power Through You
Holy Laughter
Hot Line To Heaven
How Do You Treat My Son Jesus?
How To Heal The Sick
How To Make Your Marriage Exciting
How To Overcome "Cool Down" & Keep The Fire Burning
How To Receive & Maintain A Healing
How To Receive & Minister The Baptism With The Holy Spirit
I Don't Follow Signs & Wonders...They Follow Me!
If You Really Love Me...
Impossible Miracles
Memorizing Made Easy
My Love Affair With Charles
Possessing The Mind Of Christ
P.T.L.A. (Praise The Lord Anyway!)
Since Jesus Passed By
The Fabulous Skinnie Minnie Recipe Book
Strength For Today
Supernatural Horizons (From Glory To Glory)
The Two Sides Of A Coin
This Way Up!
Video Study Guide-How To Heal The Sick (15 Hours)
Video Study Guide-How To Heal The Sick Power Pack (6 Hours)
Video Study Guide-Book of Acts (6 Hours)
Why Should "I" Speak In Tongues?

ISBN 1-878209-11-6
©Copyright 1994 by Charles and Frances Hunter, all rights reserved
Printed in U.S.A.
The Living Bible, Paraphrased, ©1971 by Tyndale House Publishers, Wheaton, IL
The New King James Version, ©1982 by Thomas Nelson, Inc., Nashville, TN
The Amplified Bible, Expanded Ed. (AMP), ©1987 by Zondervan Corporation and the Lockman Foundation

Contents

What In The World Is Going On?

Hold onto your hat - you're about to be caught up in a whirlwind that's coming your way!

There is a powerful new wind of the Holy Spirit blowing, but it's lots more than a rushing mighty wind! There's an energizing, forceful sound that's coming with this new wind of the Spirit and it is the exciting sound of joy, joy, joy, joy! Not only an inward joy, but it's bringing a vocal joy, a holy laughter, right along with it. It's energetically stirring us to higher levels with God!

The Spirit of God is swiftly moving in breathtaking and sometimes startling new ways, and people of every tongue and every nation are letting out what is on the inside of them. People of all races and denominations are radically falling in love with Jesus in a brand new way! They are running at a fast pace to "Joel's Bar" where the drinks are free and there is no hangover! The new wine is flowing and people are drinking and drinking and there is not a hangover in sight, but the results which "hang over" are spectacular!

This awesome new move of the Holy Spirit is swiftly breaking down the bonds of religion and tradition and setting people beautifully free in the Spirit!

"Behold, the former things have come to pass, and new things I declare; Before they spring forth I tell you of them" *(Isaiah 42:9)*.

"Do not remember the former things, nor consider the things of old. Behold, I will do a new thing, now it shall spring forth" *(Isaiah 43:18)*.

On that wonderful, historic Day of Pentecost, the Bible says, *"And they were all filled with the Holy Spirit and began to speak with other tongues as the Spirit gave them utterance..."* *(Acts 2:4)*. And what did the world think?

The world thought they were drunk. AND THEY WERE...gloriously drunk on the Holy Spirit! Once again God is supernaturally restoring the joy of the Lord to the church, and once again people are getting delightfully drunk on the incomparable power of the Holy Spirit!

All of the countries represented there on that wonderful inspiring day said, *"'We hear them speaking in our own tongues the wonderful works of God.' So they were all amazed and perplexed, saying to one another, 'Whatever could this mean?'*

"Others mocking said, 'They are full of new wine.'

"But Peter, standing up with the eleven, raised his voice and said to them, 'Men of Judea and all who dwell in Jerusalem, let this be known to you, and heed my words. For these are not drunk, as you suppose, since it

is only the third hour of the day. But this is what was spoken by the prophet Joel:

> *"And it shall come to pass in the last days,*
> *says God, that I will pour out of My Spirit*
> *on all flesh;*
> *Your sons and your daughters shall prophesy,*
> *Your young men shall see visions,*
> *Your old men shall dream dreams.*
> *And on My menservants and My maidservants*
> *I will pour out My Spirit in those days;*
> *And they shall prophesy.*
> *I will show wonders in heaven above,*
> *And signs in the earth beneath..."* *(Acts 2:11-19)*.

And one of today's signs "in the earth beneath" is the "holy laughter" which is supernaturally overcoming people in services all over the world!

Praise and worship has become one of the greatest parts of the church services today, and the miraculous begins to happen in praise and worship. When we say "praise and worship," we do not mean just singing where we automatically vocalize verses 1, 2 and 4 with our noses buried in a songbook. True praise and worship is where we enter into a whole new phase of loving God. It is that special time when we are completely willing to throw our entire being, body, mind, and soul into a whole new phase of loving God through praise and worship and locking everything else outside during this special time of intimacy with God and Christ Jesus.

It is the delightfully heavenly time when we put

7

everything else out of our cluttered minds, completely close out the world, the nagging problems of the day, the irritating, sandpapering situations which have come up and seem impossible to remove from our thoughts. But that's exactly what we need to do, and concentrate on drawing closer to God and increasing our relationship in passion and zeal for the Lord.

There are times in the Christian walk when we get discouraged and lose some of the fire of our love for the Lord, at least let it burn less brightly. The same thing could be true in marriage if we are not constantly rekindling that flame to keep it burning brightly! Renewing and refreshing our passion for the Lord is a real must in the world today!

"But the hour is coming, and now is, when the true worshipers will worship the Father in spirit and truth; for the Father is seeking such to worship Him. God is Spirit, and those who worship Him must worship in spirit and truth" (John 4:23,24).

Praise and worship, under the leadership of anointed ministers, can change the course of an entire meeting. It can set the stage for the great and supernatural things to happen. Not only must they be alert to what the Holy Spirit is saying, but they must also be sensitive to how the congregation is responding.

It is not only the divine privilege, but it is also a godly responsibility of every believer to fully and completely enter into the praise and worship service. This is not the time to let your mind wander around, looking to see who is coming in late, or who just sat down in front of you. It is a wonderful time not only to close out the world, but to close our eyes so that what's going on around us won't be a distraction.

"I will declare Your name to My brethren; in the midst of the congregation I will sing praises to You" *(Heb. 2:12)*.

We should always enter the church with anticipation of what supernatural thing is going to happen to us today. When we enter into church, we should *"Enter into His gates with thanksgiving"* *(Psalm 100:4)!* When your car enters the parking lot, you're entering the gates and you ought to begin to thank God. Thank God for your church. Thank God for the parking place. Thank God for the pastor. Thank God for the worship service. Thank God for the awesome thing He is going to do to you in the next hour or so. Thank God for everything!

Then the Scripture tells us to *"Enter into His courts with praise."* When you enter into your actual church, break out in praise to God. Praise Him for your salvation. Praise Him for your health! And if you're not healthy, praise Him for your healing! Praise Him for what the Word says about your finances, *"My God shall supply all your need according to His riches in glory by Christ Jesus"* *(Phil. 4:19)*. As you enter into His courts, praise Him for everything you can think of, and then ask Him to remind you of some of the things you can't even think of, or haven't thought of in a long time.

9

Sometimes we have to get rid of a lot of our religious hang-ups when we begin to enter into the joy and the praise and worship of God. Sometimes we cannot even begin to fathom other people, but one of the things which we have learned to do is not to judge other people by what they are doing. It may seem strange — it may seem different to us, but if it's of God and God is speaking to them, let's just go right along with them because the same wild exciting thing might happen to us!

We must press in with our spirits and sing and praise God with our whole spirit, soul and body. We should totally and completely lose ourselves in His presence! Our consuming passionate love for God should be expressed by ministering unto the Lord with all of our energy, our voices, our bodies and our whole hearts. Nothing should interfere with our complete praise and worship of God.

"I will praise You with my whole heart;
Before the gods I will sing praises to You.
I will worship toward Your holy temple,
And praise Your name
For Your lovingkindness and Your truth"
(Ps. 138:1,2).

Praise and worship can and does bring the surprisingly supernatural in many ways!

Recently a friend of ours had been informed by the doctors that cancer had returned to her body. This news is not excitedly received by anyone, and there is a natural fear which occurs and grips our hearts. Is

God going to heal me again...is it going to be fatal this time? What is going to happen to me? What is going to happen to my husband (or wife)? Many thoughts enter our minds at a time like that.

She gave the problem to God, which many of us do, and then we have a tendency to take it back and worry about it some more, but at the next church service she attended, she so sought the presence of God that she was literally unaware of anything around her or in her body except the Spirit of God in the praise and worship. She said she felt she had literally stepped into the very presence of God, and then she heard that soft, beautiful, comforting voice of the almighty God. He said, "Are you standing in My presence?" She said, " Yes, Lord."

He ever so gently and sweetly asked her, "Can cancer live in My presence?"

She replied, "No, Lord, cancer cannot live in Your presence." She was instantly healed of all the symptoms which had come back on her and the cancer was gone!

During a service in Brazil, we had just ministered the baptism with the Holy Spirit and about 50,000 people spoke in tongues for the first time. The praise and worship to God was almost unbelievable at that time.

The people were so aware that what they had received was the priceless gift of the Holy Spirit, that they continued to pray in tongues without ceasing! They were very vocal and powerful in their praise to

God and we could not stop them! I held up my hand to encourage them to stop praying in tongues so we could continue with the rest of the service, but they thought I was waving at them, so they just waved back and continued praying in tongues even louder!

I said to Charles, "Honey, we've just lost the service!" I felt so far as we were concerned, we had completely lost control of the meeting. The people continued in their fervent praying in tongues.

I asked Charles what we should do and he was as uninformed as I was about how to bring the audience under control. We decided, "If you can't beat them, join them!" So we started praying in tongues as loudly as the audience.

We asked God, "What shall we do now?" And it seemed as if God had not heard us because we got absolutely nothing but a deafening silence from heaven. We could not pick up a single thing in the Spirit that God was telling us to do.

That's a horribly terrifying moment for two evangelists whose minds suddenly went blank where God was concerned with over 60,000 people in the audience !

That wasn't it at all! God knew exactly what He wanted to do and how He wanted to demonstrate His awesome power. The service in Brazil was conducted in Portuguese, and suddenly we heard a lot of screams and all the people seemed to be saying the same thing. We asked our interpreter what they were saying because there was tremendous activity on one side of the soccer field and the crowd seemed to be running after someone!

Our interpreter informed us that the audience was screaming, "Look at the man in the orange shirt!" Because people in foreign countries often have different expressions than we North Americans do, I thought that might mean something like, "He's got a yellow streak down his back," meaning the man is a coward.I asked what that meant and they told us to watch the man who was wearing an orange shirt and running as fast as he could...followed by hundreds of people in the congregation!

The "orange shirt" continued to run until he got to the platform where he breathlessly said, "God healed me and I'm not even a Christian! But I want to be saved!" The pastor on the stage immediately led him to the Lord, and then we asked what his problem had been.

What a shock to all on the platform! His answer was, "I broke my spine four years ago in an automobile accident and I've been paralyzed ever since, but during praise and worship I realized that I could stand up, and when I stood up, I knew I could walk. When I walked, I knew I could run, so I began running, praising God because He had given me a new spine while they were praising Him in tongues!"

What rejoicing we did on the stage, and as we told the entire audience what had happened, they went wild with excitement to see the awesome thing God had done because they had been obedient to what

Jesus had said in Mark 16: *"And these signs will follow those who believe...they will speak with new tongues."*

They had been obedient to the words of Jesus, and God had performed a sign and a wonder because of it - a paralyzed young man had received a new spine! We never did get to do any preaching that night because we had ministered salvation and the baptism with the Holy Spirit first, and when God began to do the supernatural, He never stopped. People got out of wheelchairs, off of stretchers, passed their crutches up to the front of the crowd and the supernatural continued until the last person had left the soccer field that night. Because they had been willing to be intense in their praise and worship of God, God's presence had so enveloped this young man that he was completely healed and God put a brand new spine in him!

Don't ever underestimate the power in praise and worship!

God might be doing a lot of things we don't understand in the natural, but remember that we don't need to understand everything He does. Let's just enjoy it!

One Hurdle After Another

I was the world's wildest sinner before I got saved, and when I was completely transformed by the grace of God in the twinkling of an eye, I became just as wild a Christian! I immediately became a spiritual pig...I wanted every single thing God had and more! I avidly read the Bible morning, noon and night whenever I had even one spare moment. If there was only time for one little verse, I crammed it into my very being! I was hungry, hungry, hungry!

I loved to sing "Blessed assurance, Jesus is mine," and I always had to raise my right hand as high as I could get it because I had that blessed assurance that Jesus had come into my heart to stay. I had no problem getting that one hand up, but when Charles and I were married and we began to nibble around where the Holy Spirit was concerned, we saw "those" people with both hands raised! One hand might not be a problem, but to us "non-Pentecostals" that second hand can weigh two tons when you try to get them both up at one time!

Whenever you begin to nibble, however, sooner or later you're going to get caught! In our nibbling around, we sneaked into a meeting of the Pittsburgh Charismatic Conference years and years ago. We had heard so many bad things about the Pentecostals, we had to have a tremendous "spiritual pig" attitude or we would never have ventured so close to that meeting. Years prior to that I would go a mile out of my way so as not to drive by a Pentecostal church just because I was so afraid of them!

I had heard that they always took you into the basement and the things that went on down in that basement were too awful to repeat sometimes! Isn't it amazing how we can believe what the devil says? Probably the thing that we feared the most, however, was the fact that we heard (and believed) that they took you down into the basement, surrounded you with a group of those "evil people" who hit you on the head and continued beating you until you moaned and groaned and someone finally said, "She's got it!" Of course, you immediately agreed with them because you would have said anything just to get them to stop because the beating was so hard and the pain so great!

The meeting we went to was very interesting because they did a thing they called "singing in tongues." We both thought it was the most beautiful thing we had ever heard in our lives. We went home and tried to show our daughter what it sounded like, but when you do it in the flesh, it doesn't sound at all like it does in the Spirit! She wasn't impressed at all!

They did insist, however, that you raise both hands, and what a struggle we had. Instead of the usual flamboyant lifting of one arm, we fought against two heavy hands which weighed a ton apiece. We finally did get them to wrist level that night, but it was no higher than that, and it was such a difficult battle because a real weight problem seemed to exist in our arms. Everyone else seemed to enjoy it, and we were glad they were singing with their eyes shut, because they couldn't see the squirming we were doing trying to participate at least a little bit!

Finally the singing stopped and they allowed us to sit down. What a relief! Surely they didn't lift both hands while they were seated! There wouldn't be room that way. They didn't, so we relaxed and listened to one of the most powerful messages we had ever heard in our entire lives. Maybe it wasn't the message that was so powerful, it was the way it was delivered! No screaming, no yelling, but speaking with a power we had never felt or experienced before in a service.

We enjoyed every minute of it and decided those Pentecostals weren't as bad (maybe) as they had been portrayed to us, but then the speaker ruined the entire evening when he said, "Those of you who want to receive the baptism with the Holy Spirit and speak in other tongues, please go right through the door behind me down into the BASEMENT!" Then we knew it was true — everything we had heard about the Pentecostals and what they did below that first floor!

We had seated ourselves right at an exit sign, and when the speaker said what he did, we got out of that place before anyone ever reached the basement door. We ran out of the building as fast as we could, and when we got to "safety," we breathlessly said, "God

17

was really protecting us, wasn't He, when He let us sit by the exit sign!" We were relieved that we hadn't been trapped by those Pentecostals, and confident of the fact that God had protected us.

And another hurdle to cross...

In our travels around the United States teaching seminars on how to be filled with the Holy Spirit without speaking in tongues, we began to hear a lot about a woman named Kathryn Kuhlman, and the things we heard about her were also unbelievable!

One positive thing we did hear was that people got healed in her services which we thought was wonderful because we have always had a compassion for the sick, but we heard that the minute they got healed, she "pushed them down on the floor!"

What was this peculiar, unspiritual thing that made her push them all down? We rejected it, of course, but our hungry little "spiritual pig" hearts drew us to one of her meetings the next morning after the experience at the Charismatic Conference.

We were shocked to discover that the church was filled two hours before the service started, but more shocked to discover there were about 2,000 people outside the First Presbyterian Church trying to get in, and we were two of them. We both knew there was no way we could get in.

We stood there for a while, however, when suddenly an usher came up and said, "Charles and Frances Hunter, are you here?" We couldn't believe our own ears - the usher knew our names! How was this possible? We later found out that Miss Kuhlman had heard that there was an "author" in the crowd and she asked that we be seated in one of the front rows. I had written only two books at the time, God Is Fabulous (my personal testimony), and Go, Man, Go! Yet somehow, she had heard we were there.

They took us in and sat us down on the very second row. Again at this service the praise and worship was wonderful, and everything we had heard about this woman was true. We saw people healed of all kinds of diseases, and just like everyone had told us, she knocked them all down as soon as they were healed.

I wondered which kind of gimmick she used to accomplish this, and yet I was also aware of the fact that there was a power present we had never seen or felt before! Miss Kuhlman came down an aisle and pointed to a man in the row across from us. He stepped out in the aisle and promptly fell down. I looked to see what she had in her hand. Surely it was some kind of an electrical "charger" which was hidden in the sleeves of her beautiful, flowing dress. I started looking at the man on the floor and looked up to see what she had in her hand that caused this to happen, and discovered the longest finger I had ever seen was pointed right at me! She crooked it, motioning for me to step into the aisle.

I immediately wondered what I had gotten myself into now, but when I looked at her, even though she was tall, she was so slender and probably weighed about half what I did, that I decided there was no way she could push me over. Somewhere, though, in the very deepest recesses of my soul there was a thought that flashed, "God, if this is of You, I want to know what it is!" That hunger in my heart would not be submerged by what I had heard about this woman pushing people over.

I stepped into the aisle. She merely said, "Jesus, bless my sister," and bless me He did! Faster than you can blink an eye, I was lying on my back on the floor of the First Presbyterian Church in my very best dress. I was picking up all the dust on the marble floor and even if I was on the way to speak at a meeting I could have cared less. I'm not sure I felt anything at that particular moment. I don't remember any "spiritual goose pimples" raising up ten feet tall, and I don't recall the hair on my arms waving and clapping their hands! All I seem to remember is that peace which passed and surpassed all understanding flooded my soul with a love of God even greater than I had ever experienced before.

Something else happened to me in that very special moment. All the arguments I previously had about the baptism with the Holy Spirit and speaking with other tongues disappeared instantly! God knows what our greatest need is when we go under the power and He can instantly take care of it! It isn't just falling over - it's falling in love with Jesus!

After that experience, I never could think of a

single reason for not speaking in tongues, and shortly after that we both received (see story in *"The Two Sides of a Coin"*).

As soon as we received the baptism with the Holy Spirit, you couldn't keep us out of Charismatic meetings! We were complete fanatics and wanted to sit in the power of God and see the supernatural every opportunity we had!

We went to a Full Gospel Businessmen's Fellowship banquet in Houston. That was when everyone wore long formals to all their banquets, so I had on my very best one and we had a wonderful time!

When the meeting was completed, and the ministry began, many of the men were working together when I noticed that one particular man was laying hands on people and they were all "falling down" just like they did at the Kathryn Kuhlman service. Charles was busy talking to a friend and so I slipped away and ran over to watch this man until I finally got up enough courage to ask him, "How do you do that?" He asked, "Why do you want to know?" I was bubbling over and I said, "I went to a Kathryn Kuhlman service and I fell down, and now I want my husband to 'fall down' too!" I didn't even know what they called this supernatural phenomenon, but all I knew was that I wanted my husband to have the same wonderful experience I had.

The man looked very intently at me and said, "So you want your husband to 'fall down'?" Again I bubbled over, "Yes, yes, yes!" He asked where Charles was, so I took him over and again he said, "So you want

21

your husband to 'fall down'?" Again my answer was an enthusiastic "yes!" He said, "Then stand right beside him," so I snuggled up as close to Charles as I possibly could, and looked at him because I knew the man was going to give him the old "one-two" and down he would fall, but that wasn't what happened at all. The man said, "So you want your husband to 'fall down'? Well, Jesus, bless Frances!" Down I went faster than you could blink an eye, followed one second later by my precious husband! Then he joined our hands together and said, "Charles and Frances, I separate you for special service unto the Lord." It was a hallowed moment never to be forgotten!

I was really happy now that my husband had fallen down, and he very quickly got up, but when I tried to get up, I discovered that someone had obviously put some Elmer's glue or some similar substance on the floor, because I was totally unable to move. I tried to get my feet and legs moving, but nothing happened! I tried to get my shoulders off of the floor, but nothing happened!

I tried to get my hands off of the floor, but nothing happened. I couldn't believe what had happened to me, because it was physically impossible for me to move!

As if that wasn't enough, then something else began to happen which was another thing I had never experienced, nor did I understand at all!

I felt as though someone had given me a divine alka seltzer because way down deep in the very center of my being I began to feel a most peculiar type of "bubbling." The alka seltzer was working overtime because it was gurgling more than anything I had ever experienced in my life. Had I eaten something at the banquet which didn't agree with me, or what was this unusual thing that was happening?

The bubbling continued to increase and it slowly left my stomach and started upward. Little by little it crept higher and higher when suddenly it reached my throat area and was dangerously close to my mouth, then it abruptly came out of my mouth in the form of the loudest laugh I have ever heard. I had put my hand over my mouth in an effort to stifle what I knew was going to be laughter, but even though I had gotten my hand off of the floor by this time, no pressure on my mouth could keep the laughing back.

I laughed, laughed, laughed and laughed. I absolutely could not understand why I was laughing so hard, but finally decided it was because I was so excited about Charles "falling down." After about thirty minutes (but what seemed like an eternity!) I stopped laughing just as quickly as I started, and suddenly I was released from the bed of Holy Ghost glue in which I had been resting! I quickly got up off of the floor and sat down quietly for the rest of the evening.

No one said a word to me explaining what had happened to me and I felt I had really made a spectacle of myself because the laughing seemed to me as if it was completely unladylike because it was so loud! However, I felt wonderful, but I really subdued myself for the rest of the evening and tucked whatever the experience was in the most remote recesses of my mind, never realizing that it might resurface at some time in the far distant future! This was a hurdle I hadn't gotten over, but I had at least started getting over it a little bit.

The peculiar laughter was completely hidden away in my subconscious until a most unusual thing happened at one of our services in the state of Washington. It was a healing service, and after we had called one person up for healing, they were healed, and fell under the power of God. At that time about the only person we knew who had ever had people fall under the power was Kathryn Kuhlman so it was a startling thing for many people.

When the woman was "slain in the spirit" the audience gasped. Some in shock, some in amazement, some just from curiosity, but all in complete wonderment at what happened. I remember the first time it ever happened to me while I was laying hands on a man. At that time I kept my eyes closed when I prayed, but during the prayer the man slipped right out from under my hand. He just wasn't there any more! I reached around where the man had been, higher, then lower, and couldn't seem to locate him any place! Finally I opened one eye and peeked, thinking God couldn't see me if I just had one eye open, and discovered the man flat out on the floor. I was horrified! I thought I had killed him because I had prayed so hard because he was so sick! This taught me never to close my eyes again during a miracle service, but to keep them open to see what was going on.

Obviously the people had not seen much of this manifestation of the Holy Spirit, so I asked how many had never previously seen anyone fall under the power of God. Ninety-five percent of the audience raised their hands indicating they had not seen this sign and wonder previously. The Holy Spirit told us to call twenty people up from the first two rows, which we did, then laid hands on all of them, and they all fell under the power of God!

This was great, but something else happened! They did not get up! They laid on the floor just the way I did at the Full Gospel meeting!

We were so new in Pentecost at that time that we didn't know what to do, because they just weren't getting up. That same Holy Ghost glue which held me to the floor was now holding them. Charles and I decided we had to do something, so we started leading the audience in singing. We are probably the world's worst singers, so the audience joined us vocalizing at the top of their lungs to override our voices!

We sang and sang and sang and sang, and finally something else unusual happened on the floor. The lady who was third in line suddenly turned over and began pounding on the floor with the palm of her hand. Charles and I were shocked, because not only was she beating on the floor furiously, she was laughing hysterically as well.

We had both forgotten how loudly I had laughed

during that unforgettable night at the banquet and decided since everything in a service should be done "decently and in order" that we had better go down and get this stopped, whatever it was.

We raced off the left side of the stage, but before we got to her, she was on her feet, had run across the room and was literally "beating" on a woman with both of her hands as hard as she could!

We nearly fainted! We couldn't believe that anything like this could happen in one of our meetings. We feared that a riot was going to start and we knew we had to put a stop to that, so we both ran over to the woman on whom she was "beating." Before we got there, however, the woman, obviously seeing our concern, said, "Don't worry, she's all right, she's all right. She's a nurse who has had Guillain-Barré syndrome for over four years and has been unable to lift her arms. They have been hanging uselessly at her sides for four years, and while she was laughing, the power of God came all over her and she was healed. The only way she could tell me was to show me because she was still laughing so hard she couldn't talk!"

That was certainly a relief! We had been nervously "sweating it out" and when we returned to the stage, we noticed that everyone on the floor was laughing hysterically, too. But we saw a small crippled-from-birth "baby" foot grow to the normal size on a young woman.

She reported later that she had always had to buy two pairs of shoes, and now her feet were both the same length! Soon there were outbreaks of laughter all over the audience, and before long the entire audience was dissolved in laughter, so we looked at each other and said, "If you can't beat them, join them," and we both started laughing. This beautiful spirit of laughter went over the entire audience and finally stopped and they all seemed completely full of the joy of the Lord.

Suddenly the lady who was working at the book table came running down the aisle screaming and said, "I had a mastectomy last year and had my left breast removed, and while we were all laughing, God grew a new breast back on!"

After all that Charles and I could do to keep the meeting "decently and in order," all these wild things kept happening and continued throughout the evening.

We were so shocked at all the things which had transpired, and being so new in Pentecost, we wanted to talk to someone who was experienced in this area, so we called our good friend, Dr. Lester Sumrall, as soon as we got back home, carefully related all the details and then asked him if he had ever seen anything like this because we wanted to know what to do with something that was a lot bigger than we were!

Dr. Sumrall said, "What you experienced in your service is holy laughter." Then he continued, "Anything that is of God is holy and anything that is holy has power connected to it." Now we began to understand why the unusual healings took place because it was a supernatural move of God and it brought supernatural healing power with it. Hallelujah!

We saw little outbreaks of this from time to time, but we never encouraged them, possibly because we were afraid of it. We didn't quench it, but we just did not encourage it, but occasionally it would break out with just one or two persons, and we ignored it.

Hurdles come in all forms, and when you have a real spiritual hunger for the things of God, you eventually run into every one of them. I guess if we had not been so hungry and thirsty, we would not have had to get over all these hurdles, but we never gave up in our persistent, unceasing, relentless search for everything that God has.

The high hurdle of dancing!

We had made friends with some beautiful Chinese people after we received the baptism with the Holy Spirit who pastored a church very close to where we lived. They were having some special services, and invited us to attend as their personal guests. We were going to be at home, so we accepted the invitation, never realizing that we were about to be faced with another hurdle we had never heard of before.

The service was beautiful and everything was "decent and in order" until a special choir number was announced. The choir stood up, all in flowing choir robes, and began to sing, but shockingly something else began to happen. They were standing behind a small balustrade similar to what many churches formerly had, and suddenly we saw legs come out from behind the choir robes and saw people jumping up and down, obviously dancing, and I was absolutely horrified. I thought, "People don't dance in church! Why, dancing is of the devil."

Dancing is not of the devil! God is the one who invented dancing, but then the devil counterfeited it and distorted it and that's why Christians say dancing is of the devil. God invented dancing and He meant it for a good purpose.

I burst out laughing! There was nothing I could do because it was such a shocking sight to see in a church. Absolutely unnerving! To keep from embarrassing myself in front of the entire church, I picked up my Bible and hid behind the open pages. I was stifling my laugh as best I could when I decided to peek out from the bottom of the Bible. I lifted it up just enough so I could see their feet again, and they were still doing it! I took refuge again behind the pages of my precious Bible and stayed there for a little while, then took courage and peeked out again. They were still doing it!

I hid again, but the third time I came out from behind my Bible, I looked over the top and saw the faces of the people who were doing the dancing. I carefully scrutinized each and every one of them and saw exactly the same thing on everyone's smiling countenance! They were worshipping God in a way I had never seen anyone worship God. They were obviously loving God in a way I had never seen anyone openly express their love of the creator of the universe.

I thought about the people I had watched when I was a little girl in church. When they sang, "It is joy unspeakable and full of glory to serve the Lord," they all looked as if they had drunk a gallon or so of sour pickle juice before they dared to think about going to church. I saw no smiles, no joy, no glory, no nothing, except people who came to church because they thought they ought to. Church was not a place where anyone ever dared to enjoy themselves!

But this time I saw people who obviously enjoyed loving and praising and worshipping God. It was not a forced expression of anyone's emotions, it was something which was genuine and real, and it touched my heart!

On the way home in the car, I said to Charles, "Dancing can't be all bad if it makes people love God like they were!" Charles had never danced in his entire life, while I had loved dancing when I was a sinner. I would go to the country club and dance the hully gully, the frug and the twist until my legs would hurt so badly I would have to come home and sit in a bath tub of scalding water to get the cramps out of them before I could go to sleep. But dancing in a church...never...I religiously knew that I was delivered from dancing when I got saved!

But we were fascinated by what we had seen, so as soon as we got home, we went into our bedroom, shut the doors, pulled down the blinds to make sure

30

that no one could see what was happening in our bed-room, and that is where Charles Hunter learned to praise God in the dance. I will never forget that beautiful night where we sang some wonderful praise songs and Charles just yielded to the Spirit and danced and danced before the Lord! He has loved it ever since and God has lifted him into high places while praising God in the Spirit!

What about Jesus?

"After these things the Lord appointed seventy others also, and sent them two by two before His face into every city and place where He himself was about to go. Then He said to them, 'The harvest truly is great, but the laborers are few; therefore pray the Lord of the harvest to send out laborers into His harvest'"(Luke 10:1,2)

Jumping down to verse 17, we are told, *"Then the seventy returned with JOY, saying, 'Lord, even the demons are subject to us in Your name.' And He said to them, 'I saw Satan fall like lightning from heaven. Behold, I give you the authority to trample on serpents and scorpions, and over all the power of the enemy, and nothing shall by any means hurt you. Nevertheless do not rejoice in this, that the spirits are subject to you, but rather rejoice because your names are written in heaven.'*

"In that hour Jesus REJOICED in the Spirit and said, 'I praise You, Father, Lord of heaven and earth, that You have hidden these things from the wise and prudent and revealed them to babes. Even so, Father, for so it seemed good in Your sight'" (Luke 10:21).

After Jesus sent out the seventy, we are told they returned with great joy. This had to include laughing, because when you are full of joy, you are happy!

Years ago I heard a teaching on Luke 10:21 where it says that Jesus "rejoiced" in the Spirit. To rejoice in this instance means to "twirl around with reckless abandon!" Can't you just visualize Jesus with so much joy that He twirled around with reckless abandon? What a sight to behold! The Son of God, the One chosen to take away the sins of the world, is so delighted with salvation that He just relaxed and did something which is probably a big shock to a lot of people!

In checking with the man who taught on this subject, he verified what we had remembered. The Greekword for "rejoice" is "agalliao." The first part, "agan," means "much or in great measure." The second part, "hallomai," means "to jump, leap, spring up (leap up and down), to exalt greatly, a great display of joy, to jump about, 'knee slapping,' and 'belly laugh!'" You will find these facts in Strong's Concordance #21 and #242 combined.

It interested us to know that Jesus said that God had hidden these things from the wise and the prudent and revealed them to babes. Sometimes when a move of God comes along, we are so "wise" we cannot see what God is doing. It breaks my heart to hear preachers today still preaching against speaking in tongues, one of the most supernatural of all the supernatural things God does. I cannot understand how a bunch of sounds I don't understand can come out of my mouth, make a heavenly language which edifies my soul, and yet I can't understand a thing I'm saying! What a sign and wonder!

I do not understand why there is so much power in holy laughter...but it's wonderful!

Just as this new-to-us wave of "holy laughter" is in the Spirit, so dancing before the Lord is called "dancing in the Spirit," and praying or singing in tongues is called "praying or singing in the Spirit."

There always has to be a scriptural reference for whatever you're doing.

Psalm 150 certainly tells about the loud praise and worship we hear today, how we are to do it, and that dancing accompanies it!

"PRAISE the Lord!
Praise God in His sanctuary;
Praise Him in His mighty firmament!
Praise Him for His mighty acts;Praise Him
according to His excellent greatness!
Praise Him with the sound of the trumpet;
Praise Him with the lute and harp!
Praise Him with the timbrel and dance;
Praise Him with stringed instruments and flutes!
Praise Him with loud cymbals;
Praise Him with the high sounding cymbals!
Let everything that has breath praise the Lord.
Praise the Lord! "

That certainly takes care of all the things which are happening in churches today in the various forms of praise and worship, doesn't it?

Holy Laughter

This Is That...

We had seen very little of holy laughter in churches until quite recently when a young man from South Africa named Rodney Howard-Browne started having this unusual manifestation of the glory of God in his services. Pastor Karl Strader of the Carpenter's Home Church in Lakeland, Florida, started excitedly calling us and telling us about this most unusual sign and wonder which was occurring in his church.

He was extremely wound up about all this laughing, and said that he had spent six weeks on the floor of his church laughing, having the most wonderful time of his life. He encouraged us to come down and participate in this. It didn't make any sense at all to us but Pastor Strader told us that Pastors Wally and Marilyn Hickey had been there and he said that Marilyn had spent the entire time on the floor laughing. Then he shared with us how Rodney had called Marilyn to the microphone and she just laughed and laughed and then fell under the power of God without saying anything! How undignified! Richard Roberts and many others had shared the same experience. What was this?

Marilyn Hickey has been a very dear and close

friend of ours for many years, so I called her on the telephone to find out exactly the truth of what had happened. I had never heard Marilyn so excited! She shared more experiences of what had happened during Rodney Howard-Browne's meetings, not only in Florida but in Denver, as well. Not only did this happen to her, but it affected her daughter, Sarah, too! As a matter of fact, they spent the night before Sarah's wedding at Rodney's meeting, laughing! Whoever heard of such a thing? Marilyn was late getting to the meeting, and she couldn't find Sarah, but finally discovered she was on the floor in the front. What a place to spend the night before your wedding! Both of them insist it dramatically changed their lives! Marilyn even told me that during the next week while she had been sitting at her desk, laughter would just rise up within her and she would begin to laugh, sometimes while solving serious problems! A spirit of everlasting joy had been imparted to her!

We have known Marilyn for many, many years and have always known her to walk in some of the greatest integrity of anyone in the Christian world, so we knew she wasn't pretending, exaggerating, or making up a story. We knew that something had really happened to her. Because of her sincerity and integrity, in addition to Karl Strader's account of what was happening, we decided to venture down and take a look at what was really going on. We were skeptical, but if this was a new move of the Holy Spirit, we certainly didn't want to miss it.

We had been intrigued - even though skeptical - before we called Marilyn, so in late December, after ministering at Christian Retreat in Florida, we bought plane tickets to go home late in the afternoon, giving us time to attend the first day of Rodney's winter campmeeting in Lakeland.

We sat in the back of the church because we had to leave at 3:00 PM in order to catch our plane back to Houston and we didn't want to disturb the service when we left. While we didn't see any ministering, we heard a dynamic young man preach about the signs and wonders of the Holy Spirit.

Three o'clock came, and we were still there. We were so completely fascinated with what we were hearing that Charles said, "Let's stay another ten minutes!" We thought that the ministering would start then, but it didn't...he was still preaching!

Charles said, "Let's stay until 3:20!" We did, and then the time lengthened to 3:40 and we knew we had to leave or miss our plane. We had not seen nor heard any holy laughter in the service, but we felt something in our spirits concerning the presence of God which made us hungry for more.

We almost missed our flight back to Houston, and almost wished we had because of the drawing power of the Holy Spirit!

We later got an audio copy of the entire service and listened to it over and over again and finally made the great decision to go back to Lakeland, Florida, to see what this really was!

The "peanuts" fares were on then, so we took our secretary and her husband with us for two cents each! Back to Florida we went for two nights of the campmeeting. We were really "wired for action" and listened to Rodney preach a powerful, powerful sermon the first night...*but nobody laughed.* I watched Karl Strader who was sitting on the same pew we were, and he didn't laugh at all. I heard little trickles of laughter, but basically there was no laughter that night.

Rodney made a powerful altar call and more than a hundred people went forward, which was wonderful. But there was no laughter!

We had the privilege of having lunch with Rodney before the next meeting and were thrilled with the testimony of this young man. We went to the second service confident of the fact that the entire church was going to break out in laughter. Pastor Strader had told us that people would begin to laugh during the most serious moments of the service and would continue laughing. He said Rodney would just continue with his preaching and pay no attention to it.

We were impressed with the preaching which was so mightily anointed and we waited in great anticipation for the laughter to come. IT NEVER CAME! Here we had been in two services and still no laughter! We saw demonstrations of power with Rodney just pointing at people who would then fall under the power of God. We saw people trying to crawl away from the power, but they couldn't get up off the floor, and we were laughing at them, but there was no "holy laughter" to be heard.

The powerful service was about to conclude when Rodney asked the pastors and evangelists to come forward for an anointing to take this message of the great revival that is happening all over America through these "laughing" services to wherever they went. He said they should call him the "falling evangelist" instead of the "laughing evangelist" because more people fell down than laughed, but the freshness of the holy laughter has stuck with him.

The Holy Spirit stirred our hearts that this was truly God's message for this hour, so we both went forward for the impartation of this anointing. Rodney laid hands on both of us and said, "New beginnings!" We both fell under the power, but neither of us felt anything. There was no emotion, no laughter, no spine tingling sensation of having really been pounced upon by the Holy Spirit. This was something we had to receive by faith.

I am never moved by what I see, hear, feel, taste, touch or smell, but I am moved by the Word of God. While neither of us felt any emotions of any kind, we both received by faith what Rodney Howard-Browne had so graciously imparted to us. Our secretary and her husband both said they felt they had been hit with a two-by-four when Rodney laid hands on them, but we felt nothing!

The only emotion I felt while I was on the floor was a feeling of panic, wondering how I was going to get up! The floor at the Carpenter's Home Church is slanted downward from the stage to the first row, so I was in an interesting position with my feet higher than my head. At my age it is extremely difficult for me to get up from a lying position on the floor. I wondered if they were going to have to bring in a forklift or something to get me back to an upright position! Fortunately about ten of the ushers saw my plight and helped Charles get me to my feet! Praise God!

We came home from Florida with a delightful Holy Ghost feeling that God was completely changing our ministry, not taking away from what we had done in the past, but adding a huge new dimension. With that intriguing thought in mind, I made a detailed study of the supernatural things which had happened in our past, and we knew that we knew that we knew that this was the exciting message God wanted us to share at our next speaking date, which happened to be in Detroit, Michigan.

We shared some wonderful scriptures with the people as we explained what the Holy Spirit is doing today.

"Behold, the former things have come to pass,
And new things I declare;
Before they spring forth I tell you of them"
(Isaiah 42:9).

Again in Isaiah 43:18-19, God says, *"Do not remember the former things, nor consider the things of old. Behold, I will do a new thing, NOW it shall spring forth."*

Let's not look back. Let's throw away our rearview mirrors and look to the future and experience in an awesome way what God is doing!

God is saying to all of us right now that we should not look back at the revivals of old, nor at the former moves of the Holy Spirit. God is saying to look for what He is doing right now! And doing it He is! Not only here in America, but all over the world!

On the plane trip to Detroit, I had asked God to give me a special verse which would actually show that this was scriptural. Isn't it interesting how you can read a scripture over and over again and suddenly it takes on new light? I was reading in the book of Psalms when suddenly I came to 126:2-6 which says:

"Then our mouth was filled with laughter,
And our tongue with singing.
Then they said among the nations,
'The Lord has done great things for them.'
The Lord has done great things for us,
Whereof we are glad."

I looked at the previous verse and it said,

"When the Lord brought back the captivity of Zion,
We were like those who dream."

The Psalm was talking about the return of those in captivity and they were rejoicing with the joy of their salvation.

Romans 14:17 tells us, *"For the kingdom of God is not food and drink, but righteousness and peace and JOY in the Holy Spirit."*

God must think joy is important because He certainly talks about it a lot. Jesus said in John 15:11,

41

"These things I have spoken to you, that My joy may REMAIN in you, and that YOUR joy may be FULL!" He desires our joy to remain from the moment of salvation until eternity, and He wants our cup of joy to be full, not just partially full, but full all the way to the top!

So many people have completely lost the joy of their salvation, but God is restoring it to the church through holy laughter! *"Nevertheless I have this against you, that you have left your first love" (Rev. 2:4).* He is restoring our first love through this unusual sign and wonder!

My own joy started the day I was saved. I was so completely and totally overwhelmed with thanksgiving when I realized that all my sins were forgiven that my joy just bubbled up and overflowed. What a powerfully explosive thought - my sins were forgiven, all of them! I literally wallowed in the glory for weeks and realized I didn't ever want that feeling to change but I knew that something more had to be done to keep it at that level at all times.

If we want that eternal spring of joy welling up and bubbling over in us at all times, we need to get into the Word of God for a spiritual feast, take big bites and continue chewing until our souls are fat, because the real lasting, genuine joy never comes until we are spiritually fat!

I hardly know where to start with joy, because joy is such a vital and integral part of our lives. The joy of the Lord is in our house early in the morning.

The joy of the Lord is there in the midst of all problems. The joy is there late at night.

The day that I was saved, I got a completely insatiable hunger for the Word of God which has never been satisfied. I went home and read practically the whole New Testament the first afternoon I was saved! I never read so fast in all my life because I wanted to know what the promises of God were. One of the things I remember so well is where Jesus said, "*I have told you this so that you will be filled with my joy. Yes, your cup of joy will overflow*" (*John 15:11 TLB*).

I remember telling Him that I would never make Him out a liar and that my cup of joy would be full at all times. He said His joy would remain in us and our joy would be full, full, full! Complete and overflowing. Not just a little trickle of joy occasionally. Jesus wants us to have the absolute maximum joy in our lives at all times. He said it was HIS joy that would be in us, not ours!

People often ask us how we have the strength to accomplish all the things we do. Marilyn Hickey was talking to us recently after we had returned from a long trip and she said, "The joy of the Lord is your total strength, isn't it?" Then she went on to say, "You would never be able to accomplish what you do if you didn't derive your strength from the joy of the Lord."

Don't let anything steal your joy. Remember, when you have the joy of the Lord and the Holy Spirit wants you to start laughing, then you just start laughing your little heart out.

We believe that something new and so fresh is happening in the church that none of us actually understand it or know what's going to happen as a result. I do know that the devil will do his best to rob you of every bit of your joy, but remember it's Jesus' joy that you have, so don't ever let the devil steal it!

"Your JOY no one can take from you" (John 16:22b).

"And the ransomed of the Lord shall return,
And come to Zion with singing,
with everlasting joy upon their heads.
They shall obtain joy and gladness,
and sorrow and sighing shall flee away" (Is. 35:10).

I'm redeemed and you're redeemed, so everlasting joy is going to be upon our heads. God never says to us that His joy is just going to be a temporary thing. It's an everlasting joy that's going to last from now until the day Jesus comes back again or until God takes us home, whichever comes first!

More blessings are promised us because all sorrow and mourning are going to flee away. You don't have to be sad. You don't have to be in mourning. In the midst of all your problems, there can be tremendous, tremendous joy.

"Let the heavens be glad, the earth rejoice; let the vastness of the roaring seas demonstrate his glory. Praise him for the growing fields, for they display his greatness. Let the trees of the forest rustle with praise. For the Lord is coming to judge the earth; he will judge the nations fairly and with truth!" (Psalm 96:11,13 TLB).

"Jehovah is king! Let all the earth rejoice! Tell the farthest islands to be glad" (Psalm 97:1 TLB)!

ALL of creation is going to be glad. ALL of creation is going to rejoice and that's exactly the way it should be.

"The whole earth has seen God's salvation of his people. That is why the earth breaks out in praise to God, and sings for utter joy" (Psalm 98:3-9 TLB)!

The whole earth has seen God's salvation of His people. Isn't that enough to make you break out in praise to God and sing for utter joy? I know as I've had the thrill of seeing the different members of my family come to the Lord, I can't help but just break out in praise and sing for joy. Hallelujah!

"Sing your praise accompanied by music from the harp. Let the cornets and trumpets shout!" (Psalm 98:5,6a TLB).

Glory to God! We need more loud music in our churches. Sometimes I go into a church and I feel like it's a funeral service! Praise the Lord, the Charismatic churches have come alive and they really have music that makes you want to sing and dance.

"Make a joyful symphony before the Lord, the King! Let the sea in all its vastness roar with praise! Let the earth and all those living on it shout, 'Glory to the Lord.' Let the waves clap their hands in glee, and the hills sing out their songs of joy before the Lord, for he is coming to judge the world with perfect justice" (Psalm 98:6b-9 TLB).

Can you picture in your mind what God is saying

45

here? Can you imagine the seas roaring with praise? Can you see breakers hundreds of feet high racing around the world roaring with praise? Imagine the sound of the entire living population saying, "Glory to the Lord!" All this accompanied by the waves clapping their hands and the hills singing and singing. Can you imagine the echo that might come from certain portions of hills? And probably even the fish will be flapping their flippers in praise to God!

"Make a joyful noise to the Lord, all you lands! Serve the Lord with gladness! Come before His presence with singing!" (Psalm 100:1,2, AMP).

If you make a joyful noise unto the Lord, and you serve the Lord with gladness and you come before His presence with singing, I can guarantee you that you are going to have so much joy you won't be able to contain it. And who wants to even try?

We shared all of these scriptures and of previous things which have happened in our ministry and then we asked who would like to receive a spirit of joy, and practically the entire church came forward and received a tremendous anointing for joy. The Holy Spirit told me to lay hands on the pastor and his wife which I did, and they were both so completely drunk on the Holy Spirit they could not sit in their chairs! When the pastor got up to the microphone, he was so drunk he couldn't even make his announcements!

Explosive Holy Ghost laughter filled the auditorium and the congregation experienced a joy that was unbelievable! Many people were healed of arthritis and other ailments. Some of them came forward questioning this new move of God and apparently did not receive anything as we laid hands on them, but when they got about eight or ten rows back down the aisle, the power of the Holy Spirit hit them and BAM! they fell to the floor and started laughing!

In the natural we might look at a service like this and ask, "What is the purpose of this laughter?" I don't know. I do not know. I do not know why some people, when they are touched by the power of God, will get up and be absolutely unable to talk. They sound exactly like they're drunk. As I think back on the Day of Pentecost, I remember everyone said, "These people are drunk!" And they were - drunk on the Holy Spirit and as a result their lives were never the same again!

Not one of those who was present on the Day of Pentecost and experienced the inebriating power of the Holy Spirit was ever the same. Their lives were dramatically changed and they were never carnal because they were touched with the fire of the Holy Spirit, never to return to the carnal realm again.

I believe the same thing is happening again today in this wonderful, exciting, unique revival or whatever you want to call it that is going on right now all over the world!

If you have ever seen a person who is drunk, and some of you may have even been drunk a time or two yourselves, you will notice that for the most part, people who are drunk are totally disconnected in the way they walk and talk. Many people laugh a lot when they are drunk on natural wine. The same thing occurs when you are drunk on the new wine of the Holy Spirit. We believe that God is doing something very special across the United States and all over the world where the joy of the Lord is returning to the church.

I talked with Pastor Karl Strader after we had skeptically gone to the first two meetings and asked him what the "holy laughter" actually accomplished. He told me that Rodney Howard-Browne had been in his church for a total of thirteen weeks in one year and that not one of the people on his staff would ever be the same, because their lives were changed as a result of attending the meetings.

The people of Pastor Strader's church who attended these services said that their lives were forever changed as a result of this. New commitments were made, physical and inner healings took place, and people forgave others who had wounded them.

I wrote to Pastor Wayne Jackson of the Great Faith Ministries in Detroit, Michigan, asking him to tell us what happened as a result of our sharing this holy laughter in his church.

This is what he told us:

"After you left, I told God I was a yielded vessel and wanted only what He wanted in the church, and during our praise and worship I began to walk down the aisles, asking God to do what He wanted to do.

"There were many people there who had not been at your meetings and they didn't know anything about holy laughter, but one of our 280-pound altar workers began to laugh and fell under the power of God, and before long the presence of the Holy Spirit was so strong the whole auditorium was filled with laughter. They all know the man who was rolling on the floor with holy laughter, and they knew it wasn't put on, it wasn't in the flesh, it was just totally of God!

"My wife and I received such a touch from God when you laid hands on us that my wife often breaks out in holy laughter during our services at church. She also does a lot of sewing in designing children's clothes, and she gets outbursts of laughter just while she is sewing!

"My church has never been the same and will never be the same. During praise and worship the Holy Spirit will sweep through the entire auditorium. People who have trials and tribulations are set free through this genuine holy laughter which overcomes them. The tears of this life have been blown off of people as the Holy Spirit ministers to them.

"One man who has had a terrible drinking problem was delivered during holy laughter. People drink to get away from their problems, and this man no longer has to get drunk because he has been freed by the Holy Spirit from his worry. ("And do not be drunk with wine, in which is dissipation; but BE FILLED WITH THE SPIRIT." Eph. 5:18). I believe that God is freeing the minds of the people who have had burdens.

"Most of the people in our church go to the elders and deacons when they need counseling, but we had a meeting the other night where my wife and I just sat down and shared with individuals in the church. A spirit of laughter broke out over everyone there and freedom has come into their lives!

"The first chapter of Psalms tells us that we shall bring forth fruit in its season, but while we're waiting for the due season, the laughter of the Holy Spirit can bring us joy!

"I want to repeat that my church will NEVER be the same! We thank you for coming and we want you to come back again next year!"

"But this is what was spoken by the prophet Joel:
And it shall come to past in the last days, says God,
That I will pour of out My Spirit on all flesh;
...I will show wonders in heaven above
And signs in the earth beneath" (Acts 2:17,19).

God is letting the church see signs and wonders we may never have seen before!

"And I Will Shake All Nations..."

God says and does things in the most unusual and uncomplicated ways. *"For thus says the Lord of hosts: 'Once more (it is a little while) I will shake heaven and earth, the sea and dry land; 'and I will shake all nations, and they shall come to the Desire of All Nations, and I will fill this temple with glory, 'says the Lord of hosts. The silver is Mine, and the gold is Mine, 'says the Lord of hosts. 'The glory of this latter temple shall be greater than the former,' says the Lord of hosts. 'And in this place I will give peace,' says the Lord of hosts"* (Haggai 2:6-9).

God is shaking the nations of the world in a most unique and unusual way, and it's happening everywhere! The Spirit of God is moving in breathtaking new ways and people are responding to what He is doing in unusual numbers. God is laying His powerful mighty hand on people and they are responding to something in areas where they have never fully done so before! God is reminding us that the latter glory is going to be greater than the former.

After we had shared on holy laughter the first time we went to London, England. We had never been there before and had previously planned on teaching how to minister healing to the sick, but we knew the Holy Spirit was beckoning and leading us to share what He is doing in the world today! Regardless of what happened, we knew we were to share what God is doing right now! I had plenty of sermon outlines with me, and yet I knew in my innermost being I wasn't going to use them there.

After meeting with Pastor Colin Dye for a few minutes before the service, we knew there was no turning back. He was a very serious, immaculately dressed young man with the usual reserve of the English. We fell in love with him immediately because we saw his genuine love of Jesus and for the people he pastored in the largest church in England. We also heard that there were more than 116 nations represented in his congregation, so this man was a real giant in England's Christianity. He had started 200 churches and was looking forward to starting 2,000 by the year 2,000.

I shared the history of the move of God in our ministry concerning holy laughter, and even though the English people were exceptionally warm and receptive to the message, there was nothing unusual, except their tremendous acceptance of us, until just before the end of my talk when a woman way in the back of the sanctuary suddenly was touched by the Holy Spirit and broke out in beautiful holy laughter. Not everyone is touched in this manner by the Holy Spirit during a service, but when they are, incredible things happen!

The Holy Spirit's presence was so strong I turned around to the pastor and said, "You need the same anointing for holy laughter," and with that, I simply laid my hand on top of his head! I was probably more shocked than anyone at what happened! The expression on his face changed instantly! His eyes opened wider than anyone's I have ever seen, and in less than two seconds he exploded with the greatest outburst of holy laughter I have ever heard! Genuine laughter poured right out of his innermost being. The expression was one of surprise as if he could not believe what was happening to him! He tried to stand up, but he was instantly so drunk on the power of the Holy Spirit that he couldn't stand! I lightly laid my hand on his head again, and down on the floor he went, bam!

He laughed and laughed, and rolled and rolled and tried to get up, but he was stuck with that same irresistible Holy Ghost glue which had caught me so many years before. He could do nothing but laugh and roll. He tried five times to get up off of the floor, but he never succeeded because the Holy Spirit's power was on him so strongly that he could do nothing except enjoy what God was doing in his life.

This instantly electrified the entire congregation and bursts of spontaneous laughter broke out all over the auditorium. We began to attempt to minister healing with all the laughter but discovered there is such tremendous healing power in laughter when it's holy that we didn't have to do anything except watch what

God was doing!

A woman came up on the stage with a terrible stomach problem. She was holding her stomach because it was hurting so badly, and because she was laughing so heartily when she fell under the power of God she was totally healed! She came to the microphone and reported the complete healing she received while laughing uncontrollably.

Suddenly it was as if a huge fire had started throwing off sparks which were flying in every direction. A woman who suffered for twenty years with an incurable back problem was healed and proceeded to laugh for the next thirty minutes as she was divinely glued to the floor by the Holy Ghost power.

People were healed of all kinds of diseases; lumps fell off of bodies, back problems of all kinds were healed, neck problems were instantly touched and frozen shoulders were unlocked all over the auditorium!

The Holy Spirit then directed us to have the congregation hold hands in each section and as we walked down the aisles anointing entire rows of people with the joy of the Lord, they fell under the power of God in wave after wave! What an awesome spectacle! And what laughter!

A group of twenty from Ireland had come to the meetings, and they all screamed, "We want this anointing to take back to Ireland," and what an anointing the Irish had. They kept drinking more and more of the new wine, and each drink made them more inebriated than before!

One time I asked Pastor Dye if he would like to help us minister the anointing to the Irish people, but he said, "I can't do anything but 'lauff'" (English pronunciation for laugh)...and 'lauff' he did! He absolutely could not stop, so Charles and I had to do all the anointing of the Irish people. Scottish people were there, and they took this back to their nation. Representatives from other countries were also there, and they laughingly but seriously took this back to Switzerland and Germany.

The next day the pastor told me he felt like he needed his ribs taped up because he had laughed so much, and by Easter Sunday it was impossible to get all the people into the church. The pastor had two morning services, and we started at 2 PM and continued until about 11 that night. We took a recess for about fifteen minutes around 7 PM to eat two finger sandwiches for our Easter dinner, but we had spiritual food which was much better than anything we could ever have eaten in the physical world!

It was snowing outside and we were told they had bolted the doors to keep the people out who were trying to break down the doors to get into this great move of God. They stood outside, peeking in to see what God was doing!

In our fifteen-minute break, an osteopath was brought into the pastor's study. She had a brain tumor, excruciating pain and paralysis on her forehead, and was blind in one eye. Charles ministered to her...the pain and the paralysis disappeared, and in just a few seconds, her sight returned. The power of the Holy Spirit permeated the entire building! You couldn't walk anywhere without feeling the presence of the almighty God! Later that night we saw this healed woman laughing in the Spirit!

Our teams from the United States went to minister to those in the overflow room in the basement and the same power to laugh and to heal was there. The entire church, every nook and cranny was enveloped by the power of God's Holy Spirit!

Laughters and miracles continued all day Sunday, and Pastor Dye spent most of Sunday laughing, but finally he leaped up and said, "Can I do the same thing and impart this laughter?" We anointed him to do just that and he took off! Waves of people fell under the power of God and holy laughter broke out in one of the greatest demonstrations of Holy Spirit power we have ever seen, as a liberated, anointed, power-filled pastor moved among his people in demonstration that this anointing is transferable.

Pastor Dye stood on one side of the "U" shaped balcony, pointed across to the other side of the church, and people were touched by the Holy Ghost power and fell down on the floor or in their seats laughing!

There was a sense of awe and wonder among the congregation and a feeling of mystery as to what was happening because it certainly doesn't sound very dignified or spiritual. However, what happens in the lives of the people touched by God is incredible and the important thing for which we should look.

A family reported that there had been no laughter in their house for years because of the father's bitterness. The Holy Spirit touched him and there has been constant laughter in that house ever since!

One woman reported that all bitterness in her life totally disappeared when she started laughing and she forgave all those who had hurt her. The joy of her salvation had returned to her life.

Filled to the brim with excitement because of what we had seen in London, we flew to Holland the next morning and discovered that the Holy Spirit had jumped over the English Channel and arrived before we did, or at exactly the same time, because we went to the Hague for our first service and they were expectant! Once again we spoke about the laughter that is shaking the earth!

Healings began to take place in the audience, because whenever the Word of God is preached, signs, wonders and miracles will follow. And follow they did...one person was healed of 30 years of back problems! Sometime we think a "back problem" is a small healing, but when you have been suffering in pain for many years, it's one of the biggest healings you can have!

Several people were healed of migraine headaches and their joy knew no bounds! Sicknesses of all kinds disappeared! We had prayed that Holland would receive the same touch that London had experienced, because of the extraordinary things which have been happening in the lives of people during holy laughter.

The holy laughter was there and every person in the entire audience was ministered to personally by the members of our U.S. team and the two of us. Every one of the team members saw miraculous healings!

Before we left the Hague, I went to the restroom and if there had been any question in my mind as to whether or not God had really touched the serious people in Holland, the question was settled right there! As I walked up to the ladies' room, I could hear holy laughter all over the place. When I opened the door, there were five women inside, totally consumed with the fire of God and holy laughter. After that, there was never any doubt in our minds that the same spark which had touched England had touched Holland!

The following night when we arrived at the Goed News Centrum in Rotterdam the air was electric with expectancy! News about London had traveled fast, and there were thirty people from Belgium at the meeting—they all came expecting! The head of the Hispanic churches of all Europe was there as well. When an audience comes expecting, miracles happen!

The praise and worship was fabulous, and the expectancy intensified throughout the worship. Miracles began to happen as soon as we started speaking and the power of God was present to heal!

They were hungry for miracles, hungry for the supernatural power of God, hungry for revival in Holland, hungry for laughter! Sparks began to fly once again which struck the heart of all those in attendance! Holy laughter broke out and Pastor John Howard ran up and asked us to anoint all the staff members of his church. He was so excited he couldn't even wait until the end of the service! He was so hungry he wanted that anointing "right now!"

We immediately anointed them and then they stepped out into the audience with our team members, and miracles, falling under the power of God and holy laughter broke out in every area of the church. Many who had sorrow in their lives had it wiped out by the holy laughter!

The people from Belgium, all thirty of them, rushed forward and asked to be anointed to take the spark of revival back to their country. Their hunger for the power of God caused us to know that another spark had been ignited in another nation!

One of the things which is so refreshing and thrilling about this spark of revival is that the sparks are flying so rapidly and touching so many different nations that everyone who is touched in this awesome move of God wants to take it and spread it all over the world!

God will manifest His power and His gifts wherever He is welcomed. In a life or a church where the power of God and the demonstration of His Spirit are not welcome, you will never see those things. But when God's power is welcomed into a life that is hungry to receive everything God has, you will see some of the greatest—and some of the most unusual—mani-festations of God's power that have ever been seen.

This is what God wants for your life...that your joy may be full!

Rodney Howard-Browne tells on one of his tapes that when he went back to Africa and held a four-week revival, one of the pastors came to one meeting and didn't like what he saw. He went back to his church, stood before his congregation on Wednesday night and made this announcement publicly to his church, "People, I want to tell you right now that what's hap-pening down there in that church is of the devil." He said, "What's happening down at that church is noth-ing more than a bunch of emotionalism. It's of the devil, and I don't want any of you to go over there and get involved in it," and everyone said, "Amen!"

He then opened his Bible and started to teach for a few minutes, when he fell over backwards and got stuck to the floor and started laughing uncontrol-lably. Then he managed to claw his way back and pulled himself over to the podium and looked at ev-erybody and said, "It's God, it's God, it's God, it's God!"

God has the most unique way of convincing people who cannot see that this is of Him. But praise the Lord, He is using this most unusual and extraor-dinary form of Holy Ghost signs and wonders to bring people to Him. It is amazing how many individuals who have been lukewarm up until now have discov-ered their burners turned up to high heat, and loving every minute of it!

We went to a border town in Texas and the meetings was attended by mostly Mexican nationals, many of whom were downcast because of their background and the poverty level in which many of them live. We were there for two days and the spirit of joy and laughter which broke out was unbelievable! People who looked as if they hadn't smiled in years were suddenly uncontrollably laughing! Arthritis was healed in the bodies of scores of people as they laughed, laughed and laughed!

Word got around after the first night and scores of teenagers came the second night to receive this wonderful gift of God and to be a part of it. They did not want to go home, nor did they want us to leave, because they were hungry for more, more, more.

Praise God, He is touching teenagers through a method which we may think is new and yet here's something we discovered in a book entitled *"Deeper Experiences of Famous Christians"* published in 1911 by the Gospel Trumpet Company of Anderson, Indiana.

"In one of Cartwright's camp-meetings a little preacher, fresh from the theological seminary, began to teach the inquirers at the altar, just to resolve to be a Christian and that would make them Christians. Cartwright objected to this, and sent him out into the audience to exhort. The power of God fell on a big man, weighing about 230 pounds, and he began to cry for mercy. The little preacher exhorted him to 'be composed,' but he prayed on until his soul was

61

filled with joy. Then in his ecstasy, he picked up the little preacher, and ran about with him in his arms dancing for joy. The little preacher was pale with fright, and was never seen again on the camp-ground." (p.238)

Some people cannot stand the supernatural of God, and it's a sad story when they cannot, because they miss out on everything that God's doing. Here is another experience shared in the same book:

"In another place Cartwright says: Sister S. said her whole soul was in agony for the blessing of sanctification...Suddenly God filled her soul with such an overwhelming sense of Divine love, that she did not really know whether she was in or out of her body. She rose from her knees, and proclaimed to listening hundreds that she had obtained the blessing. She went through the vast crowd with HOLY SHOUTS OF JOY, and exhorting all to taste and see that the Lord was gracious; and such a power attended her words that hundreds fell to the ground, and scores of souls were happily born into the kingdom of God that afternoon and during the night."

The Bible tells us that signs and wonders will follow the preaching of the Word, and the exciting thing about all this is the number of people who are born into the kingdom of God through this exciting phenomenon which is sweeping so powerfully through the ages into the twentieth century and going around the world!

From the same book:

"Billy Bray, after living many years as a drunken sinner, was born again and became a shining light for the Lord. Billy often literally danced for very joy. Some objected to his dancing and shouting, but Billy justified himself by referring to how Miriam and David danced before the Lord...'I can't help praising God,' he once said, 'As I go along the street I lift up one foot, and it seems to say, "Glory!" and I lift up the other, and it seems to say, "Amen;" and so they keep on like that all the time I am walking.'"

Wouldn't you love to see a world full of Christians so enveloped in the love of God and so full of the joy of their salvation that they couldn't helping praising the Lord with every step they take! Charles and I are going to start bouncing down the street saying, "Glory" on the left foot and "Amen" on the right foot and laughing all the way!

Holy Laughter

Let's Let God Be God!!!

Isn't it amazing how we try to put God in a box and limit the way He can do things? I remember before we received the baptism with the Holy Spirit, I earnestly wanted Him and His power and His miracles with the Holy Spirit, but...no tongues please! I discovered it doesn't work that way. The disciples had no power until they received the baptism with the Holy Spirit and spoke with other tongues, so why should it be any different today? It's amazing how fast your thinking changes once you jump from one side of the fence to the other!

Once you begin to walk in the supernatural you really have to be ready for anything and everything and never question the way God does it! Charles and I have had some of the most unusual things happen at our services, but once you know that you know that you know that you are following after the Holy Spirit, you just have to plunge ahead and not be too surprised or shocked at whatever God does, or how He does it or when He does it!

I cannot explain some of the awesome things which are written in this book because I believe they are beyond explanation. Recently, however, I have had one of the most unusual things happen which absolutely defies my ability to understand, but I'm not going to question God because of the unusual results which have happened.

Recently a gentleman who was in very severe pain called our office. He had tic douloureux which is often called the suicide disease because of the intensity of the pain and because there is no let up. Our receptionist came running into my office saying, "I think you'd better take this call because this man is in such pain he says he's going to commit suicide!"

Normally I cannot take all the prayer calls which come over the telephone, but when I am in the office, and it is a critical call, I do my best to take it. This one really sounded critical, so I cut short the call I had been on, and immediately talked to this man. He was desperate! He was absolutely at the end of life and at the bottom of everything. He was totally discouraged because of the intense pain he was having to endure, and nothing the medical profession could give him seemed to do any good. He was agonizing over the telephone, so I immediately began to pray.

Charles and I love going to church and never miss a meeting at John Osteen's church in Houston where we belong, when we are in town. We will often catch a super-early plane on Sunday morning to get back home in time to be back in the presence of God in our home church. We also love our own services! We thoroughly enjoy every time we speak and glory in the supernatural which we see in all of our services, some greater than others. I don't know of anyone who enjoys church more than the two of us!

...But when I pray over someone who is critically ill, I am very serious! There is not a lighthearted vein in my voice when I bind the devil in the name of Jesus. I am totally serious when I pray! This day as I commanded the devil of suicide to come out of this man, I meant business with my heart and soul.

I was excited because we had discovered a very simple way to get tic douloureaux and migraine head aches healed by commanding a divine wedge to be driven between any nerves and blood vessels which might be too close together, and as I made these commands, I was as serious as I have ever been about praying, when suddenly I heard laughter, louder than any I have ever heard in my entire life. The man broke out laughing so loudly I jerked the telephone away from my ear. My secretary, whose office is right next to mine, heard the laughter, too. She jumped up to see what was wrong. I couldn't even pray any more because the man was laughing so hard; all I could do was say, " Thank you, Jesus; thank you, Jesus, thank you, Jesus!" Finally the man managed to blurt out the words, "I got healed. I don't have any pain anymore!"

In the meantime Charles came into my office because he heard the explosive laughter which everyone else in the office could hear because the sound went up and down the hall.

After I hung up, I sat and looked at the telephone and wondered what had actually happened to this man. I was slightly bewildered because I couldn't figure out what happened. He didn't make us wait long, because he called back the next day to report that he had no pain since I prayed. He called back a week later and reported that he had had a CAT-scan and an MRI made, and they showed no signs of tic douloureaux or scar tissue on the brain! Thank you, Jesus!

I might have thought this was unusual or forgotten about it except it didn't stop there. The next day one of our partners called and asked me to pray for a girl who had been in a coma for seven weeks in the hospital. The doctor had told the mother that the end was near and it would only be a matter of hours for her to live. The mother had called our partner who was her cousin and given her the bad news. She immediately sat down, wrote our ministry a $1,000 memorial check in memory of the girl, called our office and told us about it, so she could tell her cousin at the funeral that she had given it.

I said, "Let me pray for her. Wouldn't you rather give a living memorial than a dead memorial?" She was very upset, but I began to pray, and right in the middle of my commanding the spirit of death to come out of her cousin's daughter, she began to laugh as holy laughter again broke out. When I say "holy laughter," it was that beautiful uncontrollable laughter, which comes from the Holy Spirit, and she continued to laugh and laugh and laugh right through my entire prayer.

The next day I received another call from her. She told me some exciting news! One hour after we had prayer for the girl, she came out of the coma and said, "I'm hungry. I want something to eat." The doctor said she was still irrational, and couldn't eat anything, but the girl insisted she was not in a coma, but that she was hungry, so they finally gave her something to eat.

Within 24 hours she was removed from intensive care, and 24 hours later she went home, completely healed by the power of God, and went back to work less than a week after that with absolutely no symptoms whatsoever! I told our partner she had given a living memorial to this girl!

Thank you, Jesus. Let the Holy Spirit have His way in whatever manner He chooses to heal!

For some reason or other, I did not connect these two healings and the supernatural way they happened during holy laughter until a third one happened! A lady called from the JFK Airport on Long Island, New York. She was from England and had flown over to the United States to come to Houston for us to pray for her, but she said she was in such pain and was so weak she could not make it to Houston, but she said she was going to the hospital there and would call me later. She had cancer and the doctors had told her that she was dying and there was nothing they could do for her.

I began to pray as seriously and earnestly as I know how, and commanded the spirit of cancer and the spirit of death to come out of her when suddenly on the end of the line I again heard this uncontrollable laughter which I finally began to recognize as holy laughter. I didn't do anything except to say, "Thank You, Jesus. Thank You, Jesus. Thank You, Jesus." The woman who had been in excruciating pain continued to laugh like the funniest thing in the world had just happened to her. I guess it did because finally she said to me, "Do you know, I'm healed! I do not have a pain in my body whatsoever." Then she burst out laughing again as she said thank you and good-bye.

She called me about four days later and said she was on her way back to England. She told me she had been to the hospital, they had made cancer tests of all kinds and could find not a single trace of cancer in her entire body! Thank You, Jesus!

Each of these laughters has come at a time when normally there would have been intense sorrow, and yet instead of sorrow, they all laughed! Who am I to question God?

We have not had any more of those type of calls since then, but God was showing us once again His supernatural way of doing things which might not be exactly the way we think it should be done.

We were on television in Houston right after this happened and were sharing the exciting things that happen during holy laughter, and this prompted another unusual telephone call about a week later. A woman who was watching the program said, "I don't believe that! I don't believe a thing they're saying! It's all been made up!"

It's amazing, however, what the Holy Spirit will do in circumstances like that. The woman could not forget what we said! She could not forget the holy laughter we were talking about, so she went to church and lit a candle to Mary, and as she did, she burst out in holy laughter! Not only that, she began to sing sounds and words she had never heard in her entire life as Jesus baptized her with the Holy Spirit! She said, "I believe! I believe! I believe!"

I remember years ago some Pentecostal people told us that one of their church members received the baptism with the Holy Spirit when the pilot light in her oven exploded, so for years the entire church thought that the way to speak in other tongues was to stick your head in the oven. It just goes to show He can do whatever He wants to do in whatever way He wants to do it!

Recently the world was glued to their TV sets as they watched the Olympics. I'm sure that even though we were sitting at home, some of us who live in the U.S. were cheering as some of the U.S. stars got medals at the Olympics. As I listened to all those people screaming and shouting, I thought, " That's perfectly normal. Why shouldn't we do exactly the same thing when God moves in exciting ways?"

We should enjoy everything God does, including holy laughter. We have seen services where people fell out under the power of God in whole sections of a church or auditorium. We have seen a dove "like as of fire" with a 50-foot wing span appear in an auditorium. What was the result? The entire audience flooded the altar for salvation. Don't criticize God for whatever He does or however He does it. The end result will always be for salvation of the lost, or for a recommitment of those who have grown cool! When the dove mentioned above appeared, the people began screaming, "God save me, God save me!"

If God wants to make everyone in our services turn cartwheels, that's all right with us. If He wants them to break out in dancing, that's all right with us. If He wants them to break out in laughter, and be a real holy roller on the floor, that's all right with us!

One thing that holy laughter effectively does is to get rid of religion and religious things. Let's all be willing to see what God is saying to the church today in the way of something fresh and new. Let's jump in and taste and see for ourself that the Lord is good.

"Seek the Lord while He may be found,
Call upon Him while He is near.
Let the wicked forsake his way,
And the unrighteous man his thoughts;
Let him return to the Lord,
And He will have mercy on him;
And to our God, For He will abundantly pardon.
'For My thoughts are not your thoughts,
Nor are your ways My ways,' says the Lord.
'For as the heavens are higher than the earth,
So are My ways higher than your ways,
And My thoughts than your thoughts.
'For as the rain comes down,

and the snow from heaven,
And do not return there,
But water the earth,
And make it bring forth and bud,
That it may give seed to the sower
And bread to the eater,
So shall My word be that goes forth from My mouth;
It shall not return to Me void,
But it shall accomplish what I please,
And it shall prosper in the thing for which I sent it.
'For you shall go out with joy,
And be led out with peace;
The mountains and the hills
Shall break forth into singing before you,
And all the trees of the field shall clap their hands.
Instead of the thorn shall come up the cypress tree,
And instead of the brier shall
come up the myrtle tree;
And it shall be to the Lord for a name,
For an everlasting sign that shall not be cut off.'"
Isaiah 55:6-13

Since His ways are so much higher than our ways, let's don't question how He does it!

Holy Laughter

What Are Signs And Wonders?

Jesus told us in Mark 16:17,18, "*And these signs will follow those who believe: In My name they will cast out demons; they will speak with new tongues; they will take up serpents; and if they drink any deadly thing, it will by no means hurt them; they will lay hands on the sick, and they will recover.*"

Most of us think of signs and wonders as being connected with only healing and miracles and yet the Word tells us of many different and most unusual kinds. In Deuteronomy 6:22, "*and the Lord showed signs and wonders before our eyes, great and severe, against Egypt, Pharaoh, and all his household.*"

Here we read about a totally different kind of sign and wonder. God carefully planned the plagues to deliver Israel, and He prepared Moses and Aaron for such deliverance. He told them exactly what to do, step by step. He turned the rod into a serpent and He caused Moses' rod to swallow all the rods of other gods. How would you like to be around when the stick you were carrying turned into a snake and ate up all the other snakes? It would really make you bug-eyed!

But it was a sign and wonder!

Then God gave Pharaoh cause to harden his heart after which He told Moses what to do next. He turned the waters to blood. Nasty subject, but what a sign and wonder!

Next He created millions of frogs, and then He answered prayer and destroyed all the frogs in Egypt except for those in the river. Can you imagine how you would feel if you had witnessed that sign and wonder? Frogs in your bed! Frogs in your kitchen! Frogs in your bathtub!

After that God turned dust into lice. Next He created millions of flies and then destroyed them. I hate flies and I hate lice, but this was still a sign and a wonder regardless.

He sent a very severe pestilence and all the livestock in Egypt died except for the livestock belonging to the children of Israel. Not a single animal of theirs died. This was a sign and a wonder both ways - Egyptian livestock died but the Israelites' livestock did not. How did the disease know the difference? A sign and a wonder!

But God didn't stop there. He went on to cause another sign and wonder in the land of Egypt. God had Moses take handfuls of ashes from a furnace and let Moses scatter it toward the heavens in the sight of Pharaoh. This caused boils to break out in sores on man and beast throughout all the land of Egypt. A most unusual sign and wonder!

"Then the Lord said to Moses, 'Stretch out your hand

toward heaven, that there may be hail in all the land of Egypt - on man, on beast, and on every herb of the field, throughout the land of Egypt. 'And Moses stretched out his rod toward heaven; and the Lord sent thunder and hail, and fire darted to the ground. And the Lord rained hail on the land of Egypt." (Exodus 9:22,23). An interesting note to this sign and wonder is that even though hail fell upon the entire land of Egypt, it did not fall upon the land of Goshen where the children of Israel dwelt. (Exodus 9:26). Another type of sign and wonder!

Okay, we've had blood, frogs, lice, flies, pestilence, boils and hail. How about locusts? Next God sent millions of locusts into Pharaoh's territory. He said, *"They shall cover the face of the earth, so that no one will be able to see the earth; and they shall eat the residue of what is left, which remains to you from the hail, and they shall eat every tree which grows up for you out of the field. They shall fill your houses, the houses of all your servants, and the houses of all the Egyptians - which neither your fathers nor your fathers' fathers have seen, since the day that they were on the earth to this day."* (Exodus 10:5,6).

How would you like to come home to a house full of locusts?

"They were very severe; previously there had been no such locusts as they, nor shall there be such after them. For they covered the face of the whole earth, so that the land was darkened; and they ate every herb of the land and all the fruit of the trees which the hail had

left" (Exodus 10:14,15). Then God turned a very strong west wind which blew the locusts into the Red Sea. What a sign and wonder!

Next God brought darkness for three days into all of the land of Egypt and no one moved from where he was for the entire time! *"But the children of Israel had light in their dwellings"* (Exodus 10:23).

Even after all this, God still wasn't finished. He said there would be one more sign and wonder and that would be a plague which would kill the firstborn of every Egyptian. The firstborn of the Israelites, however, would not be touched by the plague.

Finally, Pharaoh got the message and let the children of Israel go. It didn't take long, though, for the Egyptian king to change his mind and take his Egyptian army after them. Still, God protected His people from the hand of the Egyptians.

God protected the Israelites by parting the Red Sea, taking the wheels off chariots, and ultimately destroying the pursuing Egyptians. What a series of signs and wonders!

These are all signs and wonders which we have never seen, nor will we probably ever see, yet they occurred, and can only be classified as signs and wonders.

Think about Daniel in the lion's den. Would you trade places with him? Daniel said, *"I thought it good to declare the signs and wonders that the Most High God has worked for me"* (Daniel 4:2).

In Acts 14:3 we are told, *"Therefore they stayed*

there a long time, speaking boldly in the Lord, who was bearing witness to the word of His grace, granting signs and wonders to be done by their hands." The description and type of these particular signs and wonders is noticeably missing.

Again in Romans 15:19 we are told,*"In mighty signs and wonders, by the power of the Spirit of God, so that from Jerusalem and round about to Illyricum I have fully preached the gospel of Christ."*

If you will notice, most of the time when signs and wonders are mentioned, we are never told exactly what was included. Hebrews 2:4 says,*"...God also bearing witness both with signs and wonders, with various miracles, and gifts of the Holy Spirit, according to His own will."* Obviously, all the gifts of the Holy Spirit are signs and wonders, including speaking in tongues, casting out devils and healing the sick.

What about Shadrach, Meshach and Abednego when they were thrown into the fiery furnace? If that wasn't a sign and a wonder, then we've never seen or heard of one!

All of these are different events in different times and places. However, they could not be considered as being anything except signs and wonders.

Consider the earthquake which brought Paul and Silas out of jail. It had to be a sign and a wonder when the doors of the jail opened without a key!

Ken and Nancy Curtis were anointed at a Rodney Howard-Browne meeting to take the message of revival around the world - and around the world they went! In the Philippines, Singapore, Russia and Africa they shared the message of revival accompanied by tremendous laughter in each and every country, as recorded in their video titled, "The Laugh Heard 'Round The World."

Nancy sent us an incredible story of her mother and how she was healed through a happy heart! Is this any less a sign and wonder than the stories we read about in the Bible? No, just a different kind.

"The testimony of my mother's HAPPY HEART needs to be told. She was an alcoholic all her life, and her brain was seen on a CAT-scan as atrophied. She became a 'bag lady,' purse snatchers beat her up, she got arrested, broke probation, was a hit-and-run driver...she was well known in Clearwater, Florida...by the taxi drivers, police, judges, parole officers, and muggers.

"After being kicked out of several rehab programs for beating up the old patients who were in wheelchairs, after being tied to a chair in a psyche ward, after breaking her hip and becoming so senile and demented that she no longer knew me, the day finally came when God said, 'NOW!'

"I was visiting her, she had a stomach ache, and I asked if I could pray for her tummy. She said, "Sure." So I laid my hand on her stomach and said, 'Jesus, heal my mother's stomach.' Then God said, 'NOW!...lay your hand on your mother's heart and pray.'

"I could feel a strong anointing, so I laid my hand

on mom's heart and prayed this simple prayer, 'Jesus, give my mom a happy heart.'

"She looked at me and said, 'You sure talk pretty.' Remember, she didn't know who I was. Then, she folded her hands, looked up toward heaven, (she is an Irish Catholic) and said,'Jesus, now I am ready, take all of me.'

"All the way home in the car I praised God for answering my prayers.

"Two weeks later my mother's guardian called and asked, 'Nancy, what happened to your mother?'

"I asked back, 'What happened to my mother?'

"The response was, 'We thought she had a stroke, but she didn't. She has been laughing and giggling for two weeks now. She is happy all the time.'

"So I told them of my prayer, and that God must have answered it.

"When I went to see her, as soon as I walked through the door she said, 'Nancy, where have you been for so long?' She knew who I was!

" That was almost 2-1/2 years ago. Then she was in restraints, in a wheelchair, in diapers, etc. She acted like an animal, just putting her face into the plate and biting.

"Continually, since Jesus gave her a happy heart, she has been getting younger and healthier. She is no longer in restraints, no more bed rails, no wheelchair, she went to the toilet recently, by herself, she can eat with her right hand and silverware, she is still laughing, and is the favorite patient in the nursing home.

They call her the Ha Ha Lady.

"The staff loves her the best. They tell me that my mother is the only patient that they know what her past was like since I gave her guardian the book I wrote, 'Beyond Survival.' That book is my testimony, but ends before mom's miraculous healing.

"The social worker and mom's nurse say that they think it is so neat to see someone who had been so completely transformed as an answer to prayer. They are witnesses to the miracle, since they knew her when she was mean, crippled, and insane."

We are so glad God is still in the business of signs and wonders even in the 20th Century!

Jesus said, *"Unless you people see signs and wonders, you will by no means believe"* (John 4:48). We believe with all our hearts that the reason God is having so many unusual signs and wonders happen today is so that people will believe!

I thought about the water coming from the rock in the 17th chapter of Exodus. This was an exciting story when God told Moses that He would stand before him on the rock in Horeb and when he struck the rock, the water would come out of it that the people might drink. This caused me to remember a very interesting sign and wonder that happened to me many years ago in the State of Oklahoma.

I had been invited to speak at a state campmeeting. That particular year they were expecting the largest crowd ever so a new motel had been built on their property to accommodate the additional guests. Everyone was especially excited about this meeting.

A brand new well had been dug to supply ample water to the entire campmeeting group since a record-breaking number of people was expected to attend.

My plane was late arriving and after being driven another one hundred miles to reach the campground, I had to go immediately to the platform. The meeting was wonderful and the presence of the Holy Spirit was so real. I was basking in the afterglow for just a moment when one of the pastors came up to me and said, "Frances, we need you to pray!"

I said, "Great! What do you need me to pray for?" There were about four or five thousand people attending the campmeeting, but somewhere in the neighborhood of four hundred of the elders and pillars of the church were gathering around me to form a circle.

The pastor told me that the water supply had been inadequate to take care of such a large campmeeting, so they had dug a well 276 feet down into the earth. They had to dig it so deep because in that state the water doesn't run close to the surface. The well had been working beautifully, pumping sparkling clear water when suddenly it had sucked up a rock. The rock shut off the flow of water into the new motel. (That's the same thing sin does in your life - it will cut off the flow of God's power in your life!)

They had the well drillers come out and attempt to get the rock out with no success. In spite of everything they did, the only solution they could offer was to bring the pipe back up out of the ground and dig a new well, or just dig a new well, which would be very expensive because of the depth.

What they asked me to pray for shocked me! They said, "We want you to pray and ask God to get that rock out of the well!"

Do you have any idea how that puts your faith on the line? It's a simple thing to pray for something that is hundreds or even thousands of miles away, or to pray for something where an immediate answer is not needed. This was a totally different situation. You've got a well that doesn't work, a rock stuck in its pipe and no water coming out. It's moments like this when you need some divine deodorant!

The four hundred or so of the great pillars of the church had really formed a beautiful prayer circle around me because they were all going to agree in prayer. The Word of God says, "*If two of you agree on earth concerning anything that they ask, it will be done for them by My Father in heaven*" (Matthew 18:19).

As I looked out at the faces there, I did something I had never done before and I've never done since, and may never do again for the rest of my life. But I believe with my heart and soul that the Spirit of God spoke to me and I immediately obeyed.

I stood there, searching the faces of all these great men and women of the church who had been saved for maybe thirty, forty, or even fifty years longer than I had. I felt like a new baby standing there, and suddenly, very sweetly, I said, "If there are any of you in this circle who do not believe that God is going to get that rock out, *GET OUT OF THIS CIRCLE!"*

I yelled the last five words at the top of my lungs. As a matter of fact, I yelled so loud that I shocked myself...but before I go any further, I want to ask you a question. What would you have done under the circumstances?

I'll tell you what they did! I never saw such a fast moving bunch of people in my entire life! They fell out of that circle so rapidly it almost made me dizzy!

When I looked around again, I had seven people standing with me. Everyone else had jumped out of the circle! There were only seven left, so I pulled myself together and said, "Well, guys, I think we better regroup a little bit."

And that's exactly what we did. I was standing on the platform and the seven of them surrounded me. We joined hands.

I've never learned how to pray fancy prayers. It seems to me ever since I got saved I always get myself into a jam and then I have to pray so fast that I can never remember how to pray real formally with all the beautiful words. Instead, I just have to scream out to God because it seems it's always an emergency situation. How I praise the Lord that He hears my prayers and answers them!

As I looked up to God, I saw the few who were really standing with me, and the multitudes who were out in the periphery with all of this doubt and unbelief. I very simply told God the problem. I said, "God, it's Your money. You know how You want to spend it. They've had the well diggers out here. They tried to get the rock out, but they couldn't, and now they say they have to dig a whole new well." I continued, "It's Your money and You can spend it any way You want. You can give it to the well diggers, or Father, You can supernaturally get that rock out of there and that money can be used to win people to Jesus."

I waited just another second and said, "Father, I ask You in the name of Jesus to please get that rock out!"

With that last simple little sentence, I looked back at the seven, and one of them had left the circle. He had gone over to a little building which stood maybe twenty or twenty-five feet from where we were praying.

He flipped the switch to the well, and two hundred and seventy-six feet down in the earth I heard the most glorious sound I've ever heard in my entire life. *Glug, glug, glug, glug, glug, glug, glug.* Suddenly water shot out of the top of the pump exactly like it shoots out of a fire hose!

God isn't dead! The supernatural power of God is still available today to those who are willing to cross over and do what God tells them to do.

I had people ask me that day and they've asked me ever since, "Weren't you afraid?"

"No, why should I be afraid?"

"Weren't you afraid that God wouldn't get the rock out?"

Would you believe that thought never entered my mind? I just remembered that He said whatever I asked, I would have if I just believed it when I asked it. I believed with my heart and soul that when I asked Him to get the rock out that He was going to do just that!

Paul says, *"I have been crucified with Christ; it is no longer I who live, but Christ lives in me; and the life which I now live in the flesh I live by faith in the Son of God, who loved me and gave Himself for me "*(Gal. 2:20).

If we, too, have been crucified, if we are dead to self, we can never be embarrassed whether something succeeds or fails!

Truly a sign and a wonder as surely as any of the ones mentioned in the Bible. Jesus Christ is the same yesterday, today and forever! He is still continuing and will continue doing signs and wonders through those who believe and who preach the gospel to every creature.

A totally different kind of sign and wonder concerns a meeting Charles and I addressed many years ago. The story is told in the book PRAISE THE LORD ANYWAY. I want to recount it here because it is a totally different situation than we would normally think of as a sign and wonder, and yet it is!

One of our greatest joys is being able to share daily miracles that God is doing RIGHT NOW and to encourage others to find the same beautiful, but narrow road. We had been unusually blessed as the presence of God enveloped the entire room where we were sharing at an all-day retreat held high in a beautiful mountain setting. There were probably 125 people present and the quarters were very cramped. Everyone was sitting on the floor in their casual clothes, and it was a really intimate situation where the reality of Christ could be not only discussed but His very presence felt by all concerned. It was one of the most beautiful days of my life. It was about fifteen feet from the room where we were sharing to the dining room, so there was no time for privacy or talking to anyone alone, so everyone shared their burdens and joy before everyone else and it was a great time of growing for all concerned.

The windup of the retreat was a banquet which was to be over at 7 P.M. I had talked so much during the ten-hour retreat I was extremely silent during the meal and was just listening to those around me. About ten minutes till seven I realized that in just ten minutes someone would be picking us up to take us to our next speaking engagement, which was two hundred miles away, so I decided quickly that I had better excuse myself from the banquet and go to the little girl's room.

Now watch what happened! For some reason or other (you don't think it could have been God, do you?) I turned to a lady to whom I had not said a word, and asked her, "Will you please take me to the rest room?" She gave me a most startled look, but immediately got up. Now the thing that is unusual is the fact that I'm really a grown woman and perfectly capable of finding a rest room by myself, but somehow or other, God had led me to ask the woman sitting next to me to take me. We got up and left the banquet hall, and started down a long corridor which led to the dorms when she said, "I'm new here myself, and I don't know my way around, but I'll be glad to help you."

As we got part way down the hall, we discovered the rest room, which was occupied, and about ten ladies were standing outside. Now the normal thing to do would be to stand in line and be number eleven, wouldn't it? But for some reason or other (again, you don't think it could have been God, do you?) I got a brilliant idea and said, "Usually plumbing runs in a straight line and I wonder if there could be another rest room on the second floor?" Looking back, I can see it had to be God because I'm not smart enough to know anything at all about plumbing. She said, "I don't know, but I'll go with you to find out." I assured her this wouldn't be necessary, but she insisted on going along. When we got up on the second floor, we discovered sure enough there was another rest room, and this one was empty. As a matter of fact, there was no one on the entire second floor.

I went into the rest room, and when I came out, I was amazed to see the young lady still standing there. As I took one step toward her, her eyes grew bigger and bigger and BIGGER, and she began to step backwards. I took another step, and she took another step backwards, and by this time her eyes were like saucers.

I stood still, because I realized that something unusual was really occurring. She backed up as far as she could, until she ran into the wall at the end of the second floor, and as she did, she cried out, "I believe God is real!" Goose pimples ran up and down my spine! I ran toward her and said, "Of course, honey, God is real, what makes you so emphatic about this right at this particular moment?"

The following story is what she told me:

Her husband had been killed and her world caved in and she decided there was no hope where she was concerned, so she put her children to bed and told them good-bye and drove up on the top of a mountain, to die. The woods were shut down because of a forest fire, so there wouldn't be any workers up there. She was crying, cursing, saying, "Okay, God, where are You? If You care so much, where are You?"

She said she had believed there was a God ever since she first heard of Him, but had seen more of the devil's works since then and always felt she had to fight her own battles in the way she was raised, through stubbornness - not giving in, not quitting. But she was quitting when she went up on the mountain. She said, "If God had a plan for me He was going to have to get me off that mountain and make me know what the plan was."

After sitting in her car, which had run out of gas, in the subzero weather for seventeen hours, normally she would have been dead, but somehow God in His love shielded her from the cold and even though she was in an area where no one could have been expected to be, the next morning a car drove up the deserted road, saw her car covered with snow, got out, discovered the partly frozen body of a woman, and took her down to the hospital in the valley, where she recovered from the effects of the cold. God wouldn't even let her die!

Somehow or other in a way she doesn't really know, God sent someone to invite her to a retreat (the one where I was to speak) and even though she didn't want to go, she went. As Charles and I came in with our excitement about Jesus Christ, I'm sure we must have turned her off completely, talking about God's love and what He wanted to do in the life of every person there, and as she studied us, she threw out a fleece. She had sized up the situation and realized it was an impossibility to be able to talk to either of us alone, so she really put God to the test and said, "Okay, God, if You're real, let me have a chance to talk to that woman ALONE before the retreat is over." And God had taken her all the way down to the wire, because in five more minutes we would have been gone forever out of her life, but there she was, and there I was, and we were alone on the second floor of the retreat house.

About this time I heard the noise of the banquet breaking up, and I remembered her fleece to God about talking to me ALONE, so I hurriedly glanced around, saw a broom closet at one side of the hall, grabbed her by the arm and said, "Get into the broom closet so we can pray!" (After all, the Bible does say go into the closet to pray, doesn't it?)

There, amidst brooms and mops and buckets and pails, the tears of joy flooded her soul because she realized that God had answered her prayer, and she prayed and asked God to forgive her of her unbelief and she asked Jesus Christ to come into her heart. My tears really joined hers as both of us realized the awesome ability of God to whom "all things are possible."

She wrote me a beautiful letter after this happened, and I want to quote just a little part of it to you:

"When I threw out my fleece and went up on the mountain to die - I just didn't want to live the way I have for the past three years - in limbo. I felt like a big toad - doing nothing but sitting on a rock, and I was real ripe for the devil's temptations.

"A year ago I took him up on them. To quote you, 'I was sinning and loving every minute of it.' I didn't have anything else to do. I felt like I was losing my soul, because no matter what excuses I made up, I knew God did not approve of what I was doing, so I went up on the mountain, way up, as far as I could go with the little gas there was in the car. Well, God got me off the mountain. When I met you ten days later I felt like I got a little piece of my soul back.

"The next day I went over my list of sins and since I had decided my worst sin was cussing, I was standing in the shower that morning, and I did like you said, took all my nasty words, raised them up to God, opened my hand, turned it over and watched them all run down the drain (so I thought). For twenty-four whole hours not even one little cuss word slipped out.

"*I* really felt big. Thought I had the answer to all my problems - raise them up, turn them over, and watch them run down the drain. Until the next day a little word slipped out. Just a little one, didn't think God would notice. Then it got to be a couple a day. I really got disgusted with myself and figured even God couldn't help me with that dirty habit of the tongue. (I've been cussing since I was about six).

"It took me about two weeks to realize what God had really done. I was still cussing, but I hadn't spanked my kids in two weeks. Unbelievable, when you have five kids in the house. You know why I hadn't spanked them? My terrible, quick, temper was gone. That really knocked me down a peg. *I* gave God what *I* thought was my worst sin but *He* took the one *He* wanted first."

Then she closed with a marvelous statement. She wrote, "I know God will take care of the other problems – *I* can't solve them."

Think of all the different signs and wonders which had to take place before the end result that God desired was accomplished!

All of the signs and wonders mentioned in this chapter are completely different, and yet that's exactly what they are. Let's never question the way God does it, let's just praise Him because He does it!

On one of his tapes, Rodney Howard-Browne told about a most unusual sign and wonder! Not everyone gets the message of holy laughter as being a divine sign and wonder from God, and some pastors have had problems with laughter. One pastor who was very violently opposed to the holy laughter was sitting down when suddenly the Holy Ghost fell on him and he fell right out of his chair.

Then he did a very unusual thing. He pulled his tie out in front of himself, then crawled up to the end of the tie, then he repeated the act again and continued to pull the tie out, then crawl up to it. Finally his tie "led" him under the grand piano where he stayed for two-and-a-half hours. That ended his disagreement with holy laughter!

A "Frozen" Sign & Wonder

That new wine is flowing like a sparkling, fast-moving river and people are drinking deeper than ever before. More Christians are getting drunk on the Holy Spirit than anyone could ever dream possible! This new wine is filled with genuine Holy Ghost power and everyone who has tasted it is enthusiastically encouraging everyone else to join them and have another drink, and then another drink!

The world is hungry for the supernatural of God and that is the reason they are so enthusiastically and quickly jumping into this river of new wine. People are fed up with dead religion, dead church services where nothing happens, singing which is nothing but letting your mind wonder about what TV programs you're going to watch in the afternoon after the boring church service is over, what you're going to have for dinner or whether or not you should eat out.

Either the book of Acts is true or it's a lie. Either Jesus Christ is the same yesterday, today and forever, or He's not, and in spite of some of the things which have been around for years, people are hungry for a fresh touch from God. And when I say hungry, they are really hungry!

What are they hungry for? *"Indeed it came to pass, when the trumpeters and singers were as one, to make one sound to be heard in praising and thanking the Lord, and when they lifted up their voice with the trumpets and cymbals and instruments of music, and praised the Lord, saying:*

'For He is good,

For His mercy endures forever,'

that the house, the house of the Lord, was filled with a cloud, so that the priests could not continue ministering because of the cloud; for the glory of the Lord filled the house of God" (2 Chron. 5:13,14).

Would to God that our praise and worship would rise to such heights today that the house of the Lord would be filled with a cloud so that the priests could not continue ministering because of the glory of God! That's what we're hungry for, and that's what the Christian world is hungry for!

At a Texas meeting, the praise and worship was fabulous, and everyone there was lifted into the throne room of God because of it. This put everyone in the right spirit to receive all that God had for them!

The first one we called out was a woman on whom the Spirit had really fallen. She told me her husband was a pastor and that they had given up their church seven months previously, and she was praying that we would call her out. We called her husband forward too, having previously had no knowledge of who they were or what their problems were, but God knew, and that's why He let His glory shine on them first of all!

Under the Spirit they both went and they both began to bubble with holy laughter. Then we quickly called a woman up who had the glory all over her, and she fell under the power after an explosion of holy laughter, and never got up until the end of the service! She tried many times, only to discover she would fall back again and the laughter would come once again!

The glory of God continued to fall upon different people including the staff members of the church when God suddenly said, "Now is the time for imparting this anointing to the pastor and his wife!"

We called them both up, laid hands on them and imparted to them the gift of holy laughter to pass on to others, and they both fell under the power. The wife began to laugh instantly, her spirit being filled with holy laughter, and she found herself stuck to the floor in the most heavenly, divine glue you could ever imagine! Her husband was laughing at her, but he himself did not get "it" at that particular time, however, every time he tried to get up, the congregation would say, "Touch him again," and so I would and even though he would go down, the genuine laughter never came.

I never worry about this because I know if it doesn't hit them at the moment hands are laid on them, it will eventually happen, so we continued ministering to others, but turned around often to see what

was happening on the stage. The pastor was just lying there, apparently enjoying himself and watching
his wife when suddenly she tried to get up and got as
far as a "crawl" position on her hands and knees, and
then she "froze" right on the spot, completely unable
to move because of the glory of God being on her so
strongly. She remained in exactly the same position
for at least forty-five minutes. She said she felt a tremendous lightness and freedom but most important
of all, a total awareness of His presence engulfing her.

We called her a week later and asked her exactly
how she felt, and she said, "I've never been drunk in
my whole life, but I was sure drunk on the new wine
Saturday night!" She says she has no recollection of
time passing while she was frozen because it didn't
seem as though time existed. She had stepped over
into the majestic realm of the supernatural for about
an hour. Some day she will discover all God did for
her in that sacred time!

"*Girolamo Savonarola, of Italy, was one of the
greatest reformers, preachers, prophets, politicians, and
philosophers the world has ever known. After a lifetime
of preaching the gospel, 'on Christmas Eve, in the year
1846, Savonarola, while seated in the pulpit, remained
immovable for five hours, in an ecstasy, or trance, and
his face seemed illuminated to all in the church, and
this occurred several times. '"*(From *Deeper Experiences
Of Famous Christians.*) God's been doing this all along!
That was over 500 years ago!

The pastor did not receive the spirit of laughter

until the very end of the service when Charles started to take an offering for our ministry. The church was laughing so loudly it was impossible for him to be heard, so the pastor decided to help Charles. He stood up, opened his Bible to 2 Cor. 9:7 and started to read about how God loves a cheerful giver. He never got beyond the first few words! He must have taken a big gulp of the new wine and it really hit him, and not only did he laugh, he discovered he was completely incapable of reading. He got so totally intoxicated with the Holy Spirit he finally had to give up. He couldn't even stand up - he had to sit down in an attempt to read his Bible, and he couldn't accomplish a simple task which he does all the time!

You might wonder why this is happening today. *This is a sign and a wonder.* The church knows the pastor's wife and knows that when she is "frozen" on the stage for forty-five minutes that what has happened to her is real and genuine. If there was any doubt in anyone's mind, it dissipated as they watched her completely overwhelmed by the power and glory of God.

They love their pastor, and know him to be a great man of God, whose love of God and commitment is as great as anyone we know, and they knew when they saw him completely drunk on the Holy Spirit that truly this was a sign and a wonder from the almighty God Himself!

These things are happening to people in important positions because God is showing the lukewarm or the unbeliever that His power is real, genuine and for today for those who are hungering and thirsting for all that He has!

They enthusiastically told us that the meeting was completely refreshing to their membership and there is more excitement than ever before about just being a "Christian!" He says there is greater camaraderie among the staff members and greater awareness of the family of God. It has brought an unprecedented unity in his church!

It is impossible to "fake" being frozen. There is no way you can stay in one position without moving anything unless the power of God is on you. You might be an actor or an actress and be able to accomplish this for a few seconds or minutes, but it is impossible to be locked into a position for forty-five minutes or longer without it being a supernatural act of God.

After the service we were eating strawberries in the pastor's study when the worship leader came in and said, "Pastor, remember what a problem I've been having with my back, and how I've been going and going to the chiropractor to get it fixed up? Well, tonight during holy laughter, my back was completely, not just partially, but completely and totally healed!" He then proceeded to show all of us what he could do that he hadn't been able to do, and some of the things I'd never be able to do! Sunday he joyfully testified before the entire church what God had done for him as he yielded to holy laughter!

Just at the very end of this same service, a woman with a broken arm in a sling came up for prayer. She had broken it one week previously. Charles prayed and commanded the bones to go back together again and asked God to put in a complete new elbow. The lady (an accountant) fell under the power, was completely overwhelmed with holy laughter, and continued laughing and finally began to beat her "broken" arm on the floor during the laughter. On the stage, we all shuddered and said, "God, if You haven't healed her, she's really going to be in bad shape!"

The following week a fax from the lady said, "On my way home that night after the service I heard a 'popping' sound in my elbow. I quickly said a 'Thank You' prayer to God for whatever He had done in my arm. I have been back at work and even worked seventeen hours overtime the very next week. Praise God for healing!"

We have received some interesting letters since that exciting night. One came from a mother who said, "My daughter Kathryn, a nine-year-old, had the spirit of joy come over her very strongly. She was still laughing en route home. She actually not only received it for herself, but she said as soon as she got home she was going to lay hands on her older brother so he could receive that spirit of laughter!" *"Freely you have received, freely give."*

The hunger is shown in another letter, "Thank you so very much for ministering Saturday evening. It was absolutely great watching and listening to all the holy laughter. However, from my perspective, there was one major problem and that's the purpose of this letter! The problem: I didn't get it and I want it! Please pray for me to receive because I know that if the two of you agree, I will receive."

Another interesting letter said, " The first Saturday evening service at Victory Christian Center of Austin was the most spiritual event in my sixty years of life. I thought receiving my first year of sobriety chip at my local A.A. group in September, 1976, was a big event, even spiritual in some way, but Saturday, May 14, is the spiritual turning point of my life so far! Seeing the real movement of the Holy Spirit last Saturday put the events of the past sixty years into a totally new perspective, and I will never be the same."

It was interesting to see how many different ways God had used holy laughter in just one service!

What is the Purpose of Holy Laughter?

"Everyone who keeps from defiling the Sabbath,
And holds fast to My covenant—
Even them I will bring to My holy mountain
And make them JOYFUL in My house of prayer"
(Isaiah 56:6b,7).

We always need to be completely open to the move of the Holy Spirit and never be so closed that we cannot see that God might possibly be doing something so fresh and new today that there is no way our finite minds can understand it! Let's just enjoy it and not try to figure out God.

I read a magazine article by Dr. Lester Sumrall in which he made the statement, " The reason I have been in every move of God is because I have never criticized any ministry or work of God!"

The deliverance of people from a spirit of religion and religious things is just one of the wild, exciting things we see being accomplished through holy laughter.

As we began to meditate and think back and reminisce over some of our past services, we remembered occasional outbreaks of unusual laughter. We recently telephoned a young man who had attended one of our services because we remembered during the offering time he absolutely broke out in an uncontrollable holy laughter. He was laughing so hard, and he said he didn't want to embarrass us (or himself), that he took his coat off and tried to stuff the sleeve into his mouth. It didn't work. He simply laughed even louder! All it did was make his red face redder! He's blonde with very fair skin, and when he laughs exuberantly, his face really turns red, and he became redder and redder as he laughed throughout the taking of the offering. I paid no attention to him, because I knew he wasn't deliberately doing anything to disturb the offering. It was simply an uncontrollable thing.

I called this young man and asked him if he could tell me anything that had happened to him during this outbreak of laughter. I was extremely surprised at what he told me.

He said the first time he heard holy laughter was in the Carpenter's Home Church where we had our second Healing Explosion. One of his friends had literally dragged him to the meeting. He didn't want to attend, but the man with whom he shared his apartment insisted that he come. He wasn't married at the time, and he said he had so many problems upon his shoulders that he really wasn't interested in coming to anything "religious." He said he had a lot of "garbage" in his life which didn't belong there, but he could do nothing about it.

He came along just to please his friend and knew he wasn't going to get anything out of it, but once he got there, he felt the spirit of the meeting and began to perk up and enjoy it.

On the second day of our teaching others how to minister healing, we called a woman up on the stage who was sitting right in front of this young man. She was healed and when she returned to her seat, he said that I said something to her like, "Now, don't lose that healing! Don't let the devil steal it from you!" What I said wasn't funny at all, but the woman instantly broke out in laughter. She tried to hide behind the pew in front of her and then very unexpectedly people on each side of her began to laugh and disappear behind the pews. This young man sat watching this and couldn't understand what was going on, but he said that suddenly he felt a Holy Ghost wave come over him and he surprisingly started to laugh. Before long there were about thirty or forty people in that section who were completely dissolved in uncontrollable laughter.

Since the church we were in is very large, it was difficult to see everything that goes on. We were absolutely unaware of anything that had been going on in the back section where Mike was seated. He told me, "When I finally stopped laughing, I felt like someone had taken a shower head and washed me inside with that super powerful shower head!" He said, "I had a lot of things in my life that didn't belong there. God saved me and I never felt so clean in all my life as I did after that laughter."

We prayed for a wife for him, and before long he was married, and three little girls came along in rapid succession. Then a hurricane came through and destroyed their home on which they had no insurance. A problem came up in their business and he said, "I had a tremendous amount of financial pressure on me when we came to your service in St. Augustine (Florida) because my wife and I were so deeply in debt."

They were both sitting on the front row because he said, "I always love to watch the response of the audience and what you and Charles are doing up there, to see if the Spirit will speak to me." He said, "Every once in a while I would be real thrilled to know that the Spirit was saying something to me just the same as He had said it to you.

"Suddenly, as I was listening to you talk about prosperity, it was like another Holy Ghost wave overtook me, and once again I felt like I'd had a bath from the inside out!" He doesn't remember how long the laughter lasted, but it must have gone on for at least thirty minutes. "When it was over," he continued, "the pressure on me for finances was totally gone!" The laughter caused him to give his problems to God, and he is now out of debt! Hallelujah!

There are many things accomplished by the Holy Spirit when we yield and begin to laugh. We will all discover in the near future the many things which happen in a life during this supernatural laughter.

At a recent meeting in Texas, we were surprised at the number of children at this particular service. There was an unusual number of children between the ages of six and nine. We ministered as usual, and as we picked out individuals to come forward, we noticed that the glory of God was resting on the children. Their eager little faces were saying, "Touch me! Touch me!"

We selected a few to come up and they immediately burst out into holy laughter, fell under the power of God and laid there with the same outward expressions of joy that most adults have when confronted with this unusual manifestation of God.

Charles called one entire family of five to come forward. The father was the soloist for the night and had sung a song titled, "Touch Your People Once Again." And touch them, He did! All five members of that family fell under the power, and while they all began laughing, the father and his twelve-year-old son, the oldest, got real genuine holy laughter! They were so beautifully glued to the floor, it must have been at least an hour before any of them got up. While the mother and one of the children got spurts of holy laughter, the father, the oldest son and the nine-year-old daughter kept laughing the entire time!

At a recent meeting we had with Esther Ilnisky

of the Esther Network of Intercessory Prayers, whose ministry is primarily with children, she told us that the next great revival would be brought in by the children. Children in their church are prophesying at a young age and are scripturally accurate in their prophesies.

What an exciting thought! And we discovered the truth and possibility of this because the children just could not sit still in their seats until we had laid hands on them! They came up not once, but twice and even three times, saying such things as, "I haven't had enough! Give me some more!" or "Why am I resisting the Holy Spirit?" (this was from an eight-year-old boy!). Another one came up and said, "I didn't get it yet, and I'm not going home until I do!" One young man about eleven or twelve years old said, "I finally got it on the sixth try!" He wasn't going to give up until he did! He said a "holy heat" came all over his body, and then he started laughing!

They came in waves and waves until they all had holy laughter and were satisfied that they "had it!" Such a revival among children, and such hunger! It was an awe-inspiring sight to see these children with such a hunger, a hunger for God! Several received the baptism with the Holy Spirit during holy laughter and spoke with other tongues!

What was the spiritual result of this? We ended the service with praise and worship and then we went back to the book table to pack the books to take home. A nine-year-old boy went to the front of the church and preached and prophesied for about ten minutes to an audience of about twenty people! Awesome! We have heard about young children preaching and prophesying today, but this was the first real example we had ever seen! A little boy about four or five came back and said to me, "I just got saved tonight!"

The same Holy Ghost power that brings laughter is exactly the same power that brings healing. A lady came forward to report that a lump on her breast had completely disappeared during holy laughter. Another woman brought a man forward who had stuttered horribly all his life, and he was instantly delivered during holy laughter. He gave his testimony over the microphone and did not stutter one time!

A couple came in at the end of the service with a five-year-old girl. I was sitting down in a chair resting for a moment when they came forward, so I stood up and laid hands on them. The mother and father later told the pastor that their little girl had gotten so drunk on the power of the Holy Spirit that she could not walk straight and they had to pick her up and carry her out to the car!

We might all wonder and say, "What is the purpose of a five-year old getting drunk on the power of the Holy Ghost?" I can guarantee you this: that little girl's life will never be the same. She has had a touch from God that many children never receive and her life will be affected because of this until Jesus comes back.

How well I remember the day our daughter's oldest child, Charity, broke away from her mother and father at a meeting in which we were ministering and ran down the aisle as fast as her little legs could carry her. She was only three at the time, and she ran up on the stage and said, "Grandma, touch me!" She had seen people falling under the power of the Holy Spirit and it had stirred her little heart. She wanted to experience this touch from God!

She laid there absolutely motionless for at least thirty minutes, and for a three-year old to lay completely still for that long is a miracle in itself, but Charity's life was changed. At this writing, she is almost eighteen, has finished one year of college, and has never faltered in her relationship with God, nor has she ever questioned His lordship in her life! We all believe that a lot of this is due to that little heart being so receptive to God at the age of three when she responded to His touch!

The signs and wonders God is doing today may be different than filling the Egyptians' beds with frogs, but they are just as remarkable as He molds our future today with another type of sign of wonder!

An interesting sidelight is that the healing power doesn't stop when holy laughter subsides. After the service was ended, we were at the book table putting the books away when a young woman limped by with a large metal brace around her knee and upper leg.

Her husband said, "Please pray for my wife's knee; she has suffered for nine months, has been to six doctors and they cannot determine the cause of the pain."

With some leftover laughter lingering on both the husband and the wife in spite of the pain in her knee, we sat her down in a chair and, holding her feet forward, commanded the knee to be healed, the cartilage and the lubrication to be restored. Then we commanded the ligaments and tendons to return to their normal length and strength, and for the electrical frequencies to be normal and digest any damaged cells or scar tissue; then rebuking the pain in Jesus' name, asked her to say, "Thank You, Jesus" and test her knee.

As she began to bend the knee, you should have seen the expression on her face. Suddenly she shouted to her husband, "My knee is healed! There is no more pain!" Immediately after she knew she was healed, she jumped up in the air, touching the door post and broke out again in uncontrollable holy laughter. There was absolutely no pain when her feet came down hard on the floor!

Her little daughter came up about that time and when mama told her about the healing, the little girl could hardly believe it but joined the threesome in shouting and praising God and telling everyone around that God had done a miracle and she had no more pain!

Holy laughter turned into a painless knee and a spirit of joy on the whole family!

The laughter and power doesn't stop when the people leave the church! It continues into the restaurants where they go to talk about what happened during the evening.

The family of five went into Taco Cabana to have something to eat and the twelve-year old boy fell to the ground in back of their station wagon and began laughing again! He continued to laugh for over two-and-one-half hours. His mother said she was embarrassed because people were looking at him as he laughed for fifteen to twenty minutes in the restaurant. She said,"He is not the type to draw attention to himself, and I have always taught my children not to conjure up anything concerning the things of God, so I know it was real."

All the time the boy was laughing in the restaurant, he was saying, "Thank You, Jesus! Thank You, Jesus! Thank You, Jesus!"

The mother said she did not actually have holy laughter during the service, but she knew it was inside of her and would bubble up and come out when she needed it.

One of the ladies in the church said she laughed and laughed and lost all inhibitions. She tried to get up, but was pinned to the floor. She is known for her credibility, so people knew it was real!

Many years prior to this, we had met a three-star general in the Air Force, and after years of not being in contact with him or his family, they came to this meeting. His wife had called the previous day and we asked her what she knew about holy laughter and she wrote us an interesting story of which we were not aware:

"The first time we really ever saw the supernatural manifestation of the Holy Spirit was at a Charles and Frances Hunter meeting in Virginia. Dick and I had been called of the Lord, were baptized in the Holy Spirit and on fire for all God had, but Charles and Frances knew it would take a real jolt to shake us loose from the reserve of our 'Frozen Chosen' background. At that meeting, as the power poured through the place, everything broke loose and so did we. We have never been the same since.

"After we came into active ministry, the input of the Hunters was a constant delight and our paths crossed often. At one large ballroom meeting in Washington state, I found how contagious holy laughter could be. The wives of the men who were participating in the meeting were seated together on the front row to one side and there was an electric feeling of excitement as the Holy Spirit seemed to be as delighted as we were. Row after row of people who had been standing holding hands were swept off their feet as they went out under the power, healings were taking place and suddenly Frances gestured with her hand at our row. Instead of going out under the power, a very ladylike, quiet wife of one of the Field Directors became drunk. There is no other description for it. She was just like in the movies when they show a hilarious drunk who is having the time of his life. People hope to attain that with alcohol, but it doesn't work out that way.

"Being drunk in the Spirit is glorious. She began

to giggle and collapsed in her seat with knees bent funny and ankles turned the wrong way out. It looked as though she didn't have a bone in her body, but was a rag doll! We were laughing at the sight and it must have struck her as funny, too, because she began to laugh with us. Then it happened. Real laughter, deep, totally hilarious and infectious swept down the row. We all laughed and laughed until we had to hold our sides and tears flowed like a river. The facial contortions were enough to start it all off again if anybody paused for breath. I don't know how long it went on but I have never felt anything so wonderful, such a release and such shared joy!"

Caroline realized the healing effects of holy laughter and began to minister and appreciate this unusual manifestation of the Spirit of God. The inner healing which is accomplished through this is almost unbelievable. She wrote the following story, as well:

"After that, I was to encounter holy laughter on other occasions. One I remember well was a very loving looking matron who came up to me for prayer. She was timid and made her request like she hoped she wasn't being too much of a bother to God. I had to tilt my head down to catch her soft words. It seems that she was having trouble with grief, felt it wasn't Christian not to be able to overcome it, and wanted to ask the Lord to lift it. I thought maybe she was one of those who had clung to grief until, as the years go by, it bonds with you and you can't shake it.

"Many women who heard the Word for the first

time and realize that is what they have done and that it is self-defeating, came up for prayer to be set free. So I simply laid hands on her and asked God to absolutely fill her with His joy. You better believe that's exactly what He did! She went out under the power and I had stepped aside to pray for the next person when I heard the most delicious belly giggle - one that comes from way down deep inside. I looked down at her and smiled and turned back to the person I was trying to pray for only to have another bountiful laugh come bubbling up from this newly found spring of joy.

"The person I'd laid hands on and I both sort of chuckled to each other and tried to press on, but there was no way. By this time, she was really getting into it and the laughter just rolled in the most delicious waves. Well, as a rule it doesn't take a lot to get me started and so I wasn't surprised to find myself joining in until I realized that I, too, could not stop and was folding up, slapping my thigh and roaring with hilarious laughter. The person on whom I had laid hands was doing the same thing and by then the entire front two rows were drawn into it. It is contagious! People were nearly falling out of their seats with laughter!

"It finally ended by everybody just winding down and beginning to wipe their eyes and rub their aching sides. The dear little lady started to get up and two men rushed over and scooped her up and onto her feet. She and I embraced, enjoying another soft round of chuckles at the memory of anything so delightful, when she said very apologetically, 'I hope people who saw this won't think too badly of me for laughing so soon after my husband's death.' I asked her how long he'd been dead and was stunned to hear 'TWO WEEKS!!!' How can anyone describe the healing effects of holy laughter?"

In All Situations

None of us could ever dream in our wildest imagi-
nations the things the Spirit does through holy laughter.

Darlene came to one of our services with a hunger to have a baby. I always have tremendous faith for
this because of what the Word teaches about barren
women, so I laid hands on her and prayed for a baby,
and at the end I said, "If it's twins you have to name
them Charles and Frances!" Darlene said she wasn't
particularly in agreement for twins, but the audience
certainly was!

She became pregnant several months after that
and discovered she was actually carrying twins! She
and her husband went through the Lamaze training
and were prepared for a natural birth, but instead they
got a supernatural birth!

Rodney Howard-Browne had been at their
church, and she had not been able to attend any of
his meetings, but at a ministry and leaders' meeting,
the group prayed together and she received holy
laughter for the first time. It was such a blessing to
her that she decided to listen to some tapes about holy
laughter during her time in labor. She knew just how

to breathe as the contractions started, and they began just about 3 1/2 hours before delivery, but she discovered she could not obey the rules about breathing, because each time she did, she broke into holy laughter!

This happened about halfway through labor at the transition phase and lasted throughout all the labor. When a contraction came, laughter came with it, but there was NO PAIN!

The nurses in attendance said they had never seen anything like this. Two other nurses were wondering what kind of medication she had taken. The two doctors were wondering the same thing!

During labor, she fell asleep for possibly half an hour. The contractions seemed to stop for nearly an hour. During this time a shift change of nurses brought a Spirit-filled nurse on duty, and about fifteen minutes before delivery, the Spirit-filled nurse prayed. When the time for delivery came, the holy laughter relaxed her at the time when her body started tensing, but the laughter controlled her ventilation, relaxed her, relaxed her legs to the point where they were not tense any more, and this didn't allow her to hyperventilate!

She said there was absolutely no pain during the delivery! Nurses were standing out in the hall where screams normally come forth and could not believe the laughter they were hearing. They became instant witnesses to the power of God as they shared with other patients what happened to Darlene!

God might not do things exactly the way we would do them, but He certainly gets unusual results, doesn't He?

It's Transferable, too!

A couple whom we know and who are so hungry for all the things of God met us recently for a series of five meetings after having attended one service on holy laughter in another city. They wanted us to lay hands on them, and impart this gift to them, so we did and then they immediately went to work! We asked them to help us in the service, and as they laid hands on person after person, they were healed and fell under the power of God with holy laughter!

The services they attended were most unusual because many of the people were not the type you would expect to participate in a "holy laughter" service. There were many Swedish farmers there and their buxom wives, and many of them were over 65 or 70 years of age. One of the ladies who had the best time was 82, and she really got a spirit of laughter! God knows who is going to be open to receive what He's got for them, regardless of who we think is open.

A pastor who has been in Pentecost for a long time told us that many years ago this occurred in numerous services, but because of tradition and reserve, not many people would really let themselves enjoy holy laughter in the way they are today. This special new move of God is doing such an incredible job of sweeping over all denominational lines, age barriers, ethnic barriers and all "natural" barriers which the world might see but which God never notices. The Charismatic movement brought the body of Christ into a freedom which they had not enjoyed before, and each phase or wave of the Spirit has gone on to allow people to relax and enjoy God even more! This move of God is the greatest of all!

As we wrote this book, we couldn't help but marvel at the wondrous works of God, and how differently He does everything. Each and every one of these signs and wonders is a display of His originality.

I have never had difficulty believing in the supernatural because of the unique way God saved me and delivered me from alcohol.

I loved the taste of martinis! As a matter of fact, what I really loved was the olives in the bottom, but after I was saved, the desire left me completely. I was visiting with some good friends who had taught me to drink martinis but the husband didn't appreciate me since I accepted Jesus as my Savior and Lord, so he put a drink on the bar at their house and sarcastically said ,"Well, holy Josephine, I guess you've gotten so holy and pious that you wouldn't think of taking a drink, would you?"

I knew I didn't want it! The Holy Spirit had been dealing with me on this and I knew I didn't want the drink, but since I was a new Christian, I didn't know what to do, so I quickly threw a prayer up to God and said, "God, shall I drink it to be sociable?" I didn't want it.

"God shall I just hold it to be halfway sociable?"

That's compromise, and God never honors compromise!

Then I thought about the apostle Paul when he said, "Or am I not ashamed of the gospel of Jesus Christ?" I opened my eyes after that quick prayer thrown up to God and God had done a beautiful miracle right in front of my closed eyes! He had instantly turned that martini glass into a snake, the sign of evil in the Bible!

I looked up and said, "No, thank you, I don't drink!" I flew the banner of Jesus Christ, and instantly the snake was turned back into a martini.

All I knew was that God had told me very plainly that alcohol had no place in my life! I never thought about this as a sign and wonder until recently, but that's exactly what it was!

God wants to speak to His people in whatever way they need to be spoken to just so they will believe and be saved, delivered or whatever is needed in their life. All I know is that alcohol has never been a temptation from that day on and today I almost get sick at the smell of alcohol of any kind.

All of these supernatural signs are the work of the Holy Spirit and we need to be instant in season and out of season for whatever God wants to do in our lives! He's real, He's real, He's real!

God never fails

During the great National Evangelistic Census taken in 1992, we put everything we had into it to accomplish what God had told Charles to do. We often worked 16 hours a day, came home, fell in bed, too exhausted to do anything at home. Upon several occasions I had said to Charles, "Why don't we move the bed into the foyer of the house so I can just come in the door and fall into bed instead of going to the bedroom in the back of the house?" We were so utterly compelled by the Spirit of God to complete this tremendously huge job He had called us to that we had even said, "God, if it takes every penny we have to complete it, we'll do it!" Little did we realize the first time we said that what was going to happen!

We worked right up to the last minute, had the Soul-A-Thon on TV where churches called in the results of the participation and while we did not have reports of the great totals we had anticipated, it was a tremendous success, and even today we are still seeing results. One pastor recently told us, "That was the greatest thing that ever happened to my church. We had between twelve and thirteen hundred people accept Jesus on just that one day! What a blessing it was to us!"

I didn't remember any numbers that big coming in from his city, so I asked him, "Did you call that information in to the headquarters?"

He said, "No, was I supposed to?" This made us realize, of course, that many who had participated had not given us the information, but we were still happy knowing that we had been obedient to what God had told us to do!

The bills kept coming in, and coming in, and coming in from all the advertising, telephone calls, printing and shipping materials we had done, and suddenly we realized that the ministry was 100% out of funds to pay for this. We had not received the financial help we had anticipated, and we faced an indebtedness of almost $200,000 with no funds to pay the bills! Our mail peaked at exactly the same time the census was completed, and fell off to absolutely nothing. Now that the job was over, people were sending their money elsewhere.

We sent out an "opportunity letter" hoping to receive some donations, but while little ones came, no big ones did. What do you do at a time like this? We felt we had no choice except to dip into our personal funds to pay the ministry bills. Before the bills finally ceased coming in, we had withdrawn everything the two of us had saved in a whole lifetime. The ministry had no funds, we had no funds, but the bills were paid!

When Charles came in with the last $55,000 we had in the world, I said, "Let me hold the check for just one minute, will you?" I realized that at our ages (at that time a combined age of 148 years) most people have a reserve for their "old age", but I looked at the check, threw it up in the air and watched it slowly drift to the floor and said, "God, I trust you with my soul, so I certainly can trust you with my finances!" Charles came over, picked up the check on the floor and made a deposit slip to the ministry.

We went to a local cafeteria that night with enough money in our pockets to buy a bowl of soup and a piece of cornbread for each of us. We ate it and then went home and went to bed because we were completely exhausted from such an emotional day.

We snuggled up to each other and said, "This really makes you trust God, doesn't it?" I think in that special moment we never felt closer to God or to each other than we did right then. It certainly was not a joyous time in our lives, knowing that all the money we possessed in the "natural world" was gone to pay the bills of the ministry. We had no choice except to do the "right thing" and see that all the bills were paid!

There weren't too many words between the two of us, just that beautiful knowledge that we were clinging to each other and clinging to God in what could have been a traumatic time in our lives. I did say to Charles, "Please don't die, honey, because we don't have enough money to bury you."

Suddenly in a split second both of us began to laugh and laugh. We couldn't stop! We looked at each other then laughed and laughed again! If you had been in the most distant room in our house, you could have heard us! I'm also sure if you had come to the door of our house you would have heard this hysterical laughing. At this extremely critical time in our life, we weren't crying, we were laughing! God's Holy Spirit had touched us with laughter - just what we needed at that moment!

"Dear brothers, is your life full of difficulties and temptations? Then be happy, for when the way is rough, your patience has a chance to grow. So let it grow, and

don't try to squirm out of your problems. For when your patience is finally in full bloom, then you will be ready for anything, strong in character, full and complete" (*James 1:2-4 TLB*).

The wonderful God we serve knows what your needs are at all times, and at that moment when we could have been downcast and full of fear about the future, He filled our souls with heavenly medicine which caused us never to worry one single moment after that about who was going to supply all of our needs according to His riches in glory by Christ Jesus! I believe our faith in God was stronger that night than it had ever been in our entire lives, including those times when it looked as though my life might be ending through sickness, and we sang "I've Got Peace Like A River" on the way to the doctor's office after being told I had just a few days to live!

We went to sleep that night so securely wrapped in the arms of God because of what He had done to us, that we never again worried about who was taking care of whom. We knew the money would always be there for another bowl of soup!

Holy Laughter

Inner Healing
Through Holy Laughter

Twenty years ago at one of our home Bible study meetings we laid hands on Betty Tapscott, author of *Inner Healing Through Healing Of Memories* and many other books, and she fell out under the power of God. She said one of us came by and said, "Lord, keep her down!" She said it was as if something or someone's hand was on her neck, gently but firmly holding her down so she couldn't get up; like a powerful divine force holding her and making it impossible to get up.

Recently we laid hands on her again at our first meeting on holy laughter in Houston. She said she did not receive holy laughter, but since then there has been a feeling of serenity, she has felt and experienced more of a depth of Jesus, a cleansing, releasing in her spirit. There has been more of the presence of God and power in her ministry. There has been more anointing, an inner knowing, and inner power in her life.

Betty believes since we imparted to her the gift of holy laughter that many of the people she ministers to will find a release through this wonderful new manifestation of God.

Two wonderful examples of this came through a letter from Caroline Schaefer, wife of a retired three star general. The holy laughter released something on the inside of these people that nothing else did. God is using it as a tool to help a world that needs help!

"One particularly deep healing with a whole new gift of life came to one very special young woman. It was at a couple's retreat at Lake George, New York, several years ago where we had been the speakers. The next to the last day we had morning meetings where I had the women in one place and Dick was speaking to the men in another. The presence of the Lord was very strong and we had not finished what God wanted to do when the dining room staff came bustling in to set up lunch. They had their hands full with 500 couples to feed and so there was no use protesting. I simply said that I was going to walk across the drive to the main building to the first lobby I came to and resume ministry so if anybody wanted to come they could. They did and with no microphone and hardly enough places to sit, we pressed on.

" This particular young woman stood out among all the others to me every time my eyes would catch her gaze because she had the saddest countenance I think I have ever seen. It wasn't just sad but drained of any expression or life coming through from within. When she came forward for ministry she said she felt badly for her husband and two young daughters that she couldn't join in family fun and she was just a drain on the others, but she couldn't help it and didn't have the strength to fake it. It took only a few questions to ascertain that she had been severely abused as a child, not only physically but emotionally. Her husband evidently thought he could help her out of it by just being kind and loving but it hadn't done enough.

"She stood there anorexically thin and drawn, with the droop of the shoulders proclaiming her hopelessness. I felt the Jesus kind of compassion for her and prayed her through forgiveness and healing and she was getting a little brighter with each step along the way. Finally she was praising the Lord in a timidly grateful way and put her arms around my neck to thank me.

"After I had hugged her and she was turning to go I reached out my hand and placed it on her little concave tummy and said, 'Lord, she needs a full measure of your joy.' She actually smiled in return and then stood there with a bemused expression. We were all smiling encouragingly at her because we were so thrilled to see an emotion reflected in that previously vacant little face. About that time her stomach gave a noticeable little shudder and the strangest sound came from way down inside. It reminded me of what novels described as a rusty vault door squeaking open. She looked as surprised as we were and then another sound, a little more recognizable until a raspy giggle tried its wings. It really was as jerky and as uncertain as a little bird learning to fly. Then it flowed - rich, real, holy laughter. She looked startled and then embarrassed between rounds of the first ripples until she was caught up in it to that glorious place of abandon that so exemplifies this phenomenon. We were all laughing with her and tears of gratitude were in plentiful supply. I know that since it was God's gift to her that she is still flowing in His joy and it blesses me to even think of it.

"Probably the funniest scenario took place at a women's retreat in New Hampshire. I had noticed a rather young woman who was very outstanding not only because she was younger and taller than most of the women but they were obviously 'fussing over her.' They had evidently tried very hard to get her there and were determined to love her into the kingdom of God. She, on the other hand, was obviously put off by it and would physically give a shoulder shrug that brushed anyone aside who was trying to hug her. I gave it a wide berth since I am not called to rejection and avoid it if I can. As the meetings progressed and I had more of a chance to study the audience as I was speaking, I kept watching for any signs of softening. None. In fact it seemed to me that the more they tried to reach her the more determined she became to stay aloof from it all. I was praying for her and asking the Lord to woo her by His Spirit and to heal whatever the problem might be. The final night there had been quite a bit of ministry and deliverance and it was quite late when we closed up to go downstairs for some very welcome refreshment and winding down fellowship.

" Two women came to me and said that their primary target for the weekend was to get her willing to talk to me. I said, 'Fine to send her on in.' Oh, no, they wanted me to go to her, so I followed them down the hall past the dormitory type bedrooms and came to one where there were the standard two sets of double deck bunks and a chest of drawers. There was no place to sit but on the beds and that meant you couldn't sit upright. I tried to draw her out to talk to me about what she was feeling, what were her expectations of coming to the retreat and more importantly what did she want from the Lord. I was getting nowhere and the two ladies were getting restless as they could see her getting away and knew they might not get another chance to reach her. Since I had run out of anything that I knew to do, I asked her if we could just go to the Lord with it and she said something to the effect of, 'Sure, why not.'

"I began talking with the Lord, explaining that I was at my wit's end and besides that I was drained of strength and it was late and we all needed to get to bed. So would He please show me what I was to do to help this young woman? Then I couldn't believe what I heard myself saying, 'She's sitting here wondering what the h___ am I doing here in the first place.' That word is not even a part of my vocabulary! I heard a bark of laughter because that was exactly what she was thinking and to hear it said out loud to God struck her so funny that she laughed. The thing about it was

that after the first response it went into holy laughter
and she rolled on that bed and I caught it from her.
The two of us laughed until tears rolled down our
cheeks and we couldn't mop them up. The two ladies
who had brought her were horrified. They figured I
couldn't be the woman of God I was supposed to be
and the whole thing was irretrievably messed up.

"Every time we would pause in our laughing she
would say, 'How did you know that is exactly what I
was thinking?' Then the mere thought of it would send
us both off again. Another pause would then allow
me to gasp out that God already knows what we are
thinking and He wants us to be real with Him. Eventually I was able to get out that He loves us just as we
are and since that, too, sent us off into more uncontrollable laughter the two horrified witnesses were
ready to have me committed.

"I do not know how long it lasted; all I know is
that I have never felt such release nor felt the presence of the Lord more anywhere. As we were wiping
our eyes for the hundredth time and the used kleenex
was piling up, she became more normal again and
quite serious. She thought it out and said that the
reason she had come is that she really did want to
join in with the women at church who all seemed to
love each other and enjoy one another, but she just
couldn't. She had never had affection and found it
impossible to let her guard down to receive it. The
main reason she had held out during the conference
is that she knew that when God acts in a person they

invariably cry. She had survived this far in life by being tough and had made one of those childhood vows that bind us in adulthood even when we have forgotten making them. Her little chin had set in one of the rough times and she had said, 'I will never cry again.'

"I pointed out to her that the reason people cry in response to God's love or after a miracle of healing or whatever He has done in their case is that deep inside there is this tremendous release. It is part of the healing, it is a sign of cleansing when we are born again. It usually follows the baptism in the Holy Spirit, if not right at the moment, certainly within days. It seems as if the Holy Spirit is grieving with our spirit over all that has been wrong in our lives before and yet there is no grief attached to it, just this wonderful release. This knowing that it is done.

"I was able to share what God had shown me about it when I gave my heart to Him in a hospital bed of despair. He had watched as thirty years of denying my fear, pain or despair had made me determined not to cry even in private. I was afraid if I did I'd never be able to stop. Now it was flowing and flowing and all the dammed up well was let go. It was then He whispered to me not to fight it because tears are to the wounds of the spirit what blood is to the wounds of the flesh. It is a cleansing purifying agent. I was able to watch as it dawned on her what God had done to meet her where she was. He knew the need for tears and how she had steeled herself against them with contempt for those who cried. Instead, He had produced the same results with the same tears but the source that brought no hint of sadness. Instead there was healing laughter. I will never forget it nor can I ever get over God's gift to us."

When I first talked to Pastor Strader concerning coming to one of Rodney Howard-Browne's meetings, and when I asked him what the purpose of the laughter was, he mentioned over and over again the inner healing which had been accomplished through the holy laughter.

Many individuals never seem to understand that when they are born again their sins are forgiven and forgotten by the almighty God. Anything and everything we have ever done, regardless of how heinous or bloodthirsty it might have been has been remitted, and buried in the deepest sea, never to be remembered again. When I discovered that at the beginning of my walk with God, I wrote in one of my first Bibles, "If God doesn't remember it, neither do I!" I believe that freed me from ever feeling guilty about anything I had ever done before I got saved.

Possibly through a lack of understanding or teaching, many people never reach that level of freedom from guilt, and they carry their problems and former sin with them for years and years, forgetting that *He whom the Son sets free is free indeed!*" Jesus made the supreme sacrifice so that you and I would not have to remember and wallow in our past, but that we could enjoy our present, having been totally forgiven of our sins!

These are the type of individuals who are being released through an encounter with the laughter of the Holy Spirit. Feelings of guilt are eliminated by the washing of the laughter which is as good as any shower I know of. As one pastor put it, "It's not just a squirt on the outside, it's a cleansing from the inside!" Another one said, "It might not wash the outside, but it sure cleans the inside!"

There will always be those who do not understand a new move of God, nor will they accept it. Instead, they choose to criticize those who are involved in it. Some churches have had problems with some people leaving their churches because of outbreaks of holy laughter, but the following letter certainly explains what holy laughter can do in the life of a persecuted soul. What it has done to this woman is worth any persecution anyone might be exposed to:

"As I hear from you how opposition has set in because of the happenings of our church, particularly the Spirit of laughter, may I share some things I trust will encourage you to keep sharing how genuine this is?

"Having been rejected by my natural father, having an alcoholic for a stepfather, I was adopted by an older couple. They were fine Christian people and are now at home with the Lord. After a failing marriage, I had no idea what love from an earthly father was like or to have someone love me unconditionally. Through years of counseling, therapy, hospitalization, and several medications, I was diagnosed as a manic depressant.

135

"From the time I was fifteen, death and suicide consumed my thoughts. God had His hands on me, with a plan for my life because I never indulged in drugs, alcohol or gangs. Raised in a Christian home, there were moments I felt I had the right relationship with God. Even as an adult, I turned to God and asked that He walk with me through the trying times.

"Having met and married someone who has stayed with me when others would have walked away, he became my God of security and happiness. I continued to struggle not being able to transfer from my head what I knew was right - to my heart, my sensitivity to others decreased almost to nothing. What I needed was God's heart.

"I was an angry person who looked angry most of the time. Trying to convince people I was just a serious person was impossible. On August 28, 1993, God did a miraculous work in my life when I was convinced He no longer existed in my life. He loved me enough to allow me to feel so miserable, I realized it had to be all or nothing with God. Instantly, relationships were healed, feelings of rejection and anger were gone. The realization that God loves me for who I am, regardless of what I do, became the truth because I was so hungry for God to reveal Himself to me.

" The miracles continued to the night of Marilyn Hickey's service. Asking for, believing and thanking God in one breath, I received a double portion of an anointing from God. I not only received my prayer language, but the spirit of laughter as well.

"Laughing uncontrollably for 2-3 hours, I had to be carried to the car and have a designated driver for two services. I now have that unexplainable peace the world cannot understand. I excitingly wait for days ahead to see what direction God has for me.

"The anointing of God feels like sunlight being poured on the top of my head down to my feet, feeling ever so cleansed inside out. In September I received a word of knowledge from a visiting missionary that resulted in a healing for a chemical imbalance for which I was taking medication.

"If sharing any or all of this will help even one person, please feel freedom to do so. I wait on Him, His way, His direction, which is only perfected in Him and by Him. Thank you for your time." *L.P.*

No matter how deep the wound, no matter how long it has been there, God can remove it - one way or another! Today God's surgical knife is holy laughter.

Holy Laughter

What Happens After The Evangelist Leaves?

At an Idea Exchange meeting in Florida, the big question came up of what happens after the evangelist leaves. Do we continue to have holy laughter at every service, do we stop it, think it was a wonderful time we all had, and then go on to something new, or how do we handle it?

We have heard of many churches doubling and tripling in size after their people were introduced to holy laughter, and yet we have also heard of churches which lost many of their congregation because of not understanding the purpose of this great sign and wonder.

The pastor of the large Countryside Christian Center in Tampa, Florida answered the question beautifully, and we quote what he said, "I have been asked, how has it affected your church?"

Pastor John Lloyd said, "Our church will never be the same. As a pastor you want to protect the church...and there's nothing wrong with being cautious. It's not lack of faith, it's called wisdom. And you just want to check it out first. We have to do that. So it took me about a month to get to a Rodney Howard-Browne meeting. People kept telling me what was happening but there were people who did it the wrong way. Instead of doing it in love, they came and pointed a self-righteous finger at everyone. Then you say, 'Well, if this is what it does...I don't know if I want it or not.' There was so much pride and arrogance.

"So when I went to this meeting and saw that the Lord was really doing something, I had to open my spirit up to it. Then I went to several meetings and God touched my life.

"The Lord just arranged for it because in my heart God has called me not just as a pastor but as an apostle. We've planted churches and sent many missionaries from the church. That's got to be our major thrust. I knew that we could not allow it to cause division in the church, but it has to be done in a way that brings unity.

"And so I met with all of our pastors and prayed for all of them that it would happen to all of us together. God really touched all eleven pastors. They all began to move in that anointing.

"God arranged it because we didn't plan it. That was on a Wednesday and then that Friday we had an elders' retreat with 65 of our elders for a whole weekend. I taught the elders and shared with them and then we prayed for all the elders. Instead of being a divisive thing, God just touched us where it fell on the whole leadership at the same time. All 65 of them were laughing, drunk in the Spirit, and could not get up or walk. One blind man, an elder at our church, got healed. It was phenomenal!

"When we came back in the service it was like, 'Here we go,' and I felt like I was on a high dive and was off the board but the feeling was, 'Where is this going to land?' It got to the whole church and when we prayed in services there were phenomenal healings and miracles. It was even going outside the church. Healings were taking place through not only elders and pastors, but lay people. It was just a wonderful thing. We prayed in services where it wasn't just the leadership, but all the elders. We would pray over the whole church, and everywhere there were people on the floor. The same with kids. There would be 200 kids on the floor...100 high school kids on the floor. It affected the whole church.

"Two things happened. One is that there were people who couldn't handle it and left. And there were people who thought we weren't spiritual enough and every meeting had to have falling under the power with holy laughter or we hadn't had church. That's all they wanted. That's wrong, too. So they left, which is fine.

"I'm not changing the vision God gave us! The way an evangelist uses an anointing and the way a pastor or apostle is going to flow in this thing is going to be different. There's nothing wrong with that. As pastors we have to deal with things in a different way. And anything that becomes the focus, that gets us sidetracked from what God has really called us to do, can become a distraction. It takes wisdom to keep this thing steady, not just blowing a whistle, but keeping the wheels on the track. We need to make sure that the power is going into the locomotive and not just blowing whistles.

"My whole philosophy is to win them, train them, send them. Every place we went the anointing went with us. Romania and Jamaica...our church missionary teams take about twelve short term trips a year, and every place they went that happened. That same anointing, that same power. I felt like we had to bring it back a little bit to keep the church on track. We felt like we had to be open to the Spirit but at the same time bring some order, so we continued to win people to the Lord.

"I saw that there were all these wonderful things happening, but at the same time we weren't having as many visitors and people getting saved as we had before. I didn't know whether or not the people were afraid to invite their friends or just what the problem was.

"As we prayed and sought the Lord, we had a Saturday night service and two Sunday morning services, all with the same message. I felt that in those services we would pray after church for people who wanted prayer. But during the service we must continue to minister to the body, to minister to the saints, and reach out to the lost. Then in other services and on Wednesday nights we would pray for the sick and have a little more liberty. It's just to bring it in balance a little bit.

"I know every pastor is going to handle it differently. It's going to be a little different in every church. But then we really saw growth in the church. It just took off. Things really began to happen. I found out that anything we use has to be used for the cause. It can't become an end in itself. That cause is winning the lost. So as an apostle, my heart is to see the lost won overseas and here at home. That just beats in my heart. If this helps to do it, use it, but it can never become an end in itself. Then you're in trouble. We have to keep going outside the walls of the church. That's my heart and it feels good to hear other people saying the same thing. We've got to get the Word out.

"We can end up majoring on the minors instead of on the real harvest and the thrust that God wants. I believe this, too, it's not only foreign missions but home missions, it's all the same. As a church, we've always had that heart. We don't have a school here, we have a training center. It's a year missions program...for nine months they get classes and then for three months they're on the field getting training.

"I found out that nothing stirs the church like when you're moving in the will of God, the direction you're supposed to go. The more we give to missions and to ministries, the more God gives back to us. The same thing is not only true for what we are preaching to the people, 'Give and it will be given unto you,' but for the church as well. The more we give, the more God gives back to us in the church. We not only sow money, but sow people, sow elders and pastors and anyone who has a calling. Encourage them, train them, send them out!

"Even as we prepare a new sanctuary I don't want to be strapped in debt, I mean sometimes it just happens. I don't want to cut back in the missions in any way because that's my heart. Nothing can deter from that calling to win the lost and reach the world.

"It's like a kid with a new Nintendo game. That's all they play with. After a month it's like, 'I need a new one!' Some of the holy laughter in the church was flesh. It's just the novelty and the newness, but after a while for those who really want to move on with God there's a maturity that comes, and the novelty wears off. Now we're going to use this thing for the glory of God. There's nothing wrong with that novelty, it's great, it stirs things up, we need it. But in our church there's more maturity in strength and direction than there was a year ago. Let's focus on Jesus and point this in His direction!"

Another pastor spoke and said:

"When I first heard of Rodney Howard-Browne my oldest daughter attended a church in Spring Hill. They had a month of meetings and my daughter kept telling us about this guy. I'm an Assemblies of God minister so we finally got down next to the last night and we were able to sit on the front row. I was a little skeptical but I knew God was there. I saw the hunger that we've been talking about was there in the place. However, I did question some of the things that happened.

"I said, 'Well why does everybody fall,' but found out later that everybody doesn't necessarily fall out.

Those who are hungry for God usually are the ones who really respond. Then my middle daughter moved to Lakeland just about the time Rodney came to Lakeland, so both my daughters were able to be in one month of meetings where God really did something. We went down and I saw on a much larger scale how hungry people were. I said, 'This is the most wonderful atmosphere in which I could ever be.' I was raised in Pentecost. They started First Assembly of God in Eva, Alabama, when I was two years old in 1939. In the forties I saw people lying all over the floor. I saw it, but I'd never gone out under the power, so my little daughter grabbed me and said, 'Let's go, daddy.'

"We went up to the platform and Rodney Howard-Browne was just flying by the people when he touched me and I went out. I laid out about twenty minutes, and I took this back to my people, and told them about it! It opened a door for some traditional people, maybe, in the Assemblies of God who weren't quite as open as they should be to this ministry. It opened the door so that people were willing to let God be God. In fact, an evangelist came later and said, 'Why don't you just give God a CD, a "courtesy drop?" Go ahead and fall out and then let God do something for you when you get down on the floor!'

"I started preaching that. Give God a 'courtesy drop.' Let Him. Some of us are so proud that we are not willing for God to do something with us. You know, God didn't knock me down there, but I was willing to fall. And when I did, God began to do a work in me. I

145

saw the same thing in my own church. There are some people who are moving in the gifts of the Spirit among my leadership and God's just doing some wonderful things. We have probably had the greatest year spiritually that we've ever had. I still don't have big numbers, but God has been there. He's doing such wonderful things. I want to keep on giving Him 'courtesy drops.'

" We had gone to Rodney Howard-Browne meetings before any holy laughter ever came into our church. We still haven't had a lot, but some. Recently they called me down to the children's church and said, 'You'd better get down here.' My daughter laughed about an hour and a half and at first I was afraid, like, is this kid losing her mind? I'd never seen anything like it...children were lying on the floor, touched by the Holy Spirit and I was scared. I'd never seen my daughter do that before, she was only 10 years old at the time. I thought it was really amazing. Since then I've laughed my head off two or three times.

"The Lord is really working in my life. In this revival, we're not getting squirted on the outside, like a refreshing, we're getting filled to overflowing from the inside. We're not looking at the outside, we're looking for the Holy Spirit and the overflowing and I'm beginning to experience it in my life. And I haven't been so happy in all my life. Especially the last eight weeks, I can say I have had some of the best days I've ever had."

I believe every person on whom the spark falls has a hunger to take it back to their own church, city or nation. I believe we're in the greatest revival we have ever seen from all the sparks that you and I are throwing out.

Wherever you go, those sparks are going to fly! Wherever Charles and I go, they're going to fly! I believe God is creating a hunger in the hearts of people to know a living Jesus. You might as well wipe out dead religion because it was gone years ago. But I also believe that out of this dead religion you're seeing people rise up who are hungry for a living Jesus, a Jesus who can raise the dead just like He did 2,000 years ago, and a Jesus who is still doing miracles where you see the miraculous happen right in front of your eyes!

Not everyone will believe or receive this exciting move of God, but those who do not may be left by the wayside. This reminds me of an incident which happened many years ago, but is still fresh in our memory.

There have been times in our ministry when we have seen the multitudes fall out under the power of God with supernatural results. One such happening occurred in the state of Michigan at a campmeeting. We had ministered there for two nights previously and this was our final night.

Before the start of the evening service God spoke powerfully and said, "Minister to the children first." We contacted the State Superintendent who was in charge of the campmeeting and asked him if this was agreeable to him and he said it was.

We started the service about 6:30 in the evening with a short talk to the young people ranging in age from approximately six to eighteen. At the end of the talk we asked them all to say a sinner's prayer which they did. Then God spoke and said, "Go lay hands on each and every one of them."

"Then they brought young children to Him, that He might touch them; but the disciples rebuked those who brought them. But when Jesus saw it, He was greatly displeased and said to them, 'Let the little children come to Me, and do not forbid them; for of such is the kingdom of God '" (Mark 10:14).

We stepped off the stage and laid hands on the first two children. They both fell under the power! We laid hands on two more children. They also both fell under the power! We laid hands on child number five and child number six, and they both fell under the power, but none of them were getting up!

We continued walking through the tabernacle, and even outside on the grassy slopes, and the same thing happened to every child there except one! And they continued lying on the ground when *"suddenly there came a sound from heaven, as of a rushing mighty wind, and it filled the whole house where they were sitting. Then there appeared to them divided tongues, as of fire, and one sat upon each of them. And they were all filled with the Holy Spirit and began to speak with other tongues, as the Spirit gave them utterance" (Acts 2:2-4).*

It was as if they were all puppets and their bodies

were controlled by strings because at a sound unheard by those in the audience, they all lifted their hands and they all began to speak with other tongues, as the Spirit gave them utterance! Many of these five hundred children were from Baptist, Methodist, Catholic and other evangelical denominations who had never heard of speaking in tongues, but the wind of the Spirit hit them all at exactly the same time!

There was a hush that was so silent it could almost be heard as these five hundred children continued speaking in tongues with their hands lifted in the air. A sign and a wonder!

A photographer was there from the Saginaw, Michigan, newspaper and he snapped numerous pictures all over the auditorium and seven full pages of pictures plus the story appeared in the Sunday newspaper!

It was a night to remember, and we never go back to Michigan to minister but what someone reminds us of this most unusual event! We are still in touch with a number of those young people, some of whom have gone on to graduate from Oral Roberts University with honors because they were completely transformed after a personal touch from God on that memorable night.

There is a sad ending to a part of this story, however. The people would not let us leave the camp until we promised we would return the next year because they agreed they had never seen such a move of God. However, they drove us to Detroit to fly back to Houston, and before we arrived home some three hours later, they had called and cancelled the speaking request for the next year. Some of the pastors complained that they did not like such a big display of the power of God. The sad part is not that it affected any of the children, because they all knew that what happened to them was genuine and real and was of God, but did a denomination miss out on a great move of God?

A pastor recently said to me after a powerful meeting in his church, "Could it be that the great revival the church has been waiting for and has tried so hard to create through man-made efforts of big crusades, camp meetings, seminars, 'revival' meetings, and 'explosions' of all kinds will come through a unique method only God could have thought of:
HOLY LAUGHTER?

Let Go...
And Let God!

God has always given His people a choice. The children of Israel didn't *have* to follow Moses out of Egypt. Abraham didn't *have* to put Isaac on the altar. David didn't *have* to go to the palace to be Saul's minstrel. *But they did.*

Even Jesus had a choice to make. Remember when He prayed and asked God to let "this cup" pass from Him? Then immediately He made His choice to follow God's will and continue on His journey that would lead us to eternal life.

There is always a choice to be made. Either we follow God and be a part of what He is doing, or we hang back and miss out. This has been the way with every great move of God. Some jump into the river and get in the flow, while others stand on the bank refusing to jump into the water, waiting to see what will happen. Then, of course, there are those who will do nothing but criticize and point out everything that's wrong with what God is doing!

During our years in ministry we have faced many such decisions. One that comes immediately to mind is the decision we had to make once we had received the baptism with the Holy Spirit. We could have kept it quiet or we could have shouted it from the rooftops. If we told, it meant being disfellowshiped from our denomination, it would cost us thousands of dollars in book royalties which we were receiving at the time, and it would have brought cancellation of speaking dates. Really, though, there was never a choice to be made. We decided a long time ago that we would follow God and be a God pleaser instead of a people pleaser. Just as Paul said, *"For do I now persuade men, or God? Or do I seek to please men? For if I still pleased men, I would not be a servant of Christ"* *(Galatians 1:10)*.

When we wrote the book *Angels On Assignment* we ran into tremendous flack. One organization even threatened that they would spend every cent it took to ruin us if we published the book. Our faith is in God and because of that, we really don't "scare." But that could have been a very valid cause for us to question or to back away, but we didn't. We knew what God had told us to do so we followed His leading. Now, years later, we continue to see *Angels On Assignment* selling around the world, blessing people in almost every nation on earth! We simply obeyed God instead of trying to please people.

Whenever God gives something wonderful to us,

we simply cannot keep it inside. We want to share it with everyone around us! When we began sharing that we had received the baptism with the Holy Spirit and made altar calls, we literally had thousands of people come forward to receive. What could we do? If we tried to minister to each person individually we would have been there for days! God instantly told us that we did not have time to lay hands on each individual, so we learned how to minister to the multitudes. Some people said that we were "teaching them how to speak in tongues" since we didn't lay hands on every single person but remember, Jesus ministered to 120 the first time and never laid hands on any of them! It's the same principle as leading someone in a sinner's prayer. We can't do the saving and we can't do the baptizing. We CAN instruct them, however, on how to get where they want to go.

Remember when "falling under the power" or being "slain in the Spirit" was a new move of God? Many people immediately said it was of the devil. We had been invited to a big meeting where we had ministered the previous year, but this time we were told, "We don't want anyone falling down this year!" so we held back at that meeting and didn't touch people. And we were miserable! When we finished that meeting, Charles said, "We'll never do that again because we follow God, not people!"

There was a group out west who wanted us to come and minister, but they didn't want any falling under the power. We told them they would have to

153

tell God about that because we didn't have any choice in the matter. Twenty-eight of those people gathered in a circle, fervently praying that God would reveal to them what they should do. They ALL fell under the power of God! God had answered them very quickly with no room for doubt at all!

We could have held back in any of these situations. It would have been the easiest thing in the world to say, "Okay! We'll do it your way!" But we have always been determined to walk before God in integrity. That means not only listening to His voice, but obeying it, as well.

When we began ministering and teaching others how to heal the sick, the "flack bomb" exploded all over again. But why back off this time when we had never done so in the past? People told us that healing was supernatural and simply could not be taught. But isn't the Word of God supernatural? Of course it is! And people are teaching it all over the world, every day of the week! Why should healing be any different? It is, after all, the Word of God in action, being fulfilled!

We went ahead with what God had given us and today there are millions all over the world who have learned how to minister healing to the sick by the power of God in Jesus' name by reading our book and watching our video titled HOW TO HEAL THE SICK. We're not the ones who said that believers would go out and lay hands on the sick and see them recover. Jesus did! If we had held back on this teaching, how many people would have never received God's healing touch through the trained healing teams around the world? Again, we were just listening to and obeying the voice of God.

No matter what subject God has us teaching, our hearts are always toward winning the lost to Jesus. Because of that, we were not really surprised when God spoke to Charles to take an evangelistic census of the world. We knew this would be an impossibly huge task if we were to undertake it on our own. But since Jesus is in our hearts, we are never on our own.

Now, every person I know who confesses to be a Christian will tell you that he or she desires to see the world won to Jesus. But when we first started sharing about the National Evangelistic Census, you wouldn't believe how many people said it couldn't be done. There were many people who refused to even get involved because they didn't think it was possible–yet didn't Jesus tell us to pray that God would send workers into the harvest? How many times have we prayed that and then been unwilling to actually be one of those workers God wants to send? Again, the choice is ours to make.

As a result of the National Evangelistic Census, there have been literally millions of people born again in nations around the globe! Churches have exploded with growth as the new believers come to learn of God and worship Him!

And now here comes holy laughter, as controversial a move of God as any move we've ever seen.

As I consider the word "controversial," I wonder if there has ever been any move of God that didn't have people on both sides, for and against. Whatever the case, we have decided in our hearts to follow God and not worry about what people are saying.

One thing that each move of God has had in common is that each brought forth great demonstrations of the power of God in a different way for a different time. The greater the power displayed, the more controversial the move. Remember when the Charismatic Movement first began? Great power was demonstrated in churches across the nation and around the world! And those against that move of God were outraged by all this "speaking in tongues, dancing around and falling down!" Yet during the Charismatic Movement we saw God restore the operation of the gifts of the Holy Spirit to the church, we saw God drop His power back into His people!

This new move of holy laughter is sure to be controversial because it is so completely powerful. The lives of those who are touched in this move of God have been so radically changed that it is impossible not to believe that God is "doing something very special!"

Since we first saw holy laughter manifested in our meetings, we have seen increased healings as God's Holy Spirit supernaturally swoops down delivering healing to person after person in services where no one has personally ministered healing. God's glory is displayed in this dramatic and dynamic release of His power, clearly expressed in setting people free.

How could we question that this is God?

Of course, God expects us to use wisdom and discernment in our lives and our walk with Him. One of the greatest "acid tests" is looking for the fruit that is produced in the lives of the people involved in any move like this. Any move that is truly of God will produce lasting results that will line up with His Word. We received fax letters from Belgium and Holland recently (just in time to include in this book) in which the following comments were made concerning the meeting we held in Holland:

"We will never forget the presence of the Holy Spirit which made Jesus so real to us. The holy laughter was new to us, but we have not enough words to describe what happened. We know for sure that we received a special anointing that has made us whole. We will never be the same again. This experience has changed our lives and we are now experiencing a breakthrough in Belgium!"

The second fax said, "During the services with Charles and Frances about holy laughter, I experienced something very special. When Frances called me to come and receive, I saw fire coming out of her hand that touched me and I fell to the floor. It was very obvious, and I've never been the same since. When we went back home that evening, my heart was filled with such a supernatural joy and since that time I have more power to go through life than ever before!"

The Dutch pastor said, "The holy laughter services with Charles and Frances Hunter in Rotterdam was a tremendous breakthrough for our ministry. When they started to share about this new dimension in the spirit realm, we could just sense the electricity in the air!

"During those meetings many were healed and delivered during holy laughter. Those who wanted to come from the audience and 'lose their dignity' were touched by the supernatural finger of God Himself. Everywhere people were lying on the floor, joyfully laughing and praising God. Many were set free from spirits of religion and tradition as the power and joy of the Holy Spirit took over."

Each time the two of us have been faced with choosing to follow God into a new move, we seem to find ourselves right out on the cutting edge. Each time we must choose whether we will retreat and stay where it's "comfortable," or just throw our hands up in the air, shout "Hallelujah!" and dive right into the flow of God. If you know anything about us at all, you can guess which way we always choose to go! If not, let's just say that we're always ready to jump for Jesus! But we can't decide for anyone but ourselves. Every pastor, every church, every denomination, every believer must make up their own mind to follow God or to "wait and see."

Where will this new move go? No one knows but God, but it's obviously going all over the world. *"For the earth will be filled with the knowledge of the glory of the Lord, as the waters cover the sea" (Habakkuk 2:14)*. People who have been nominal Christians have a new and burning desire to be more like Jesus. The Word of God says, *"Be holy, for I am holy"* *(I Peter 1:16)* and there is a supernatural desire set aflame in multitudes who find themselves totally released from self and desiring to know Him!

Could this be the way God is bringing us into the final great revival before the return of Jesus? Whether it is or not, we can feel the Holy Spirit moving - and we're going right along with Him! Don't stick your toe in to test the water! Don't wait! Jump all the way into this flowing river!

Let's follow God into the greatest and most powerful move ever seen in the history of the church! Listen and you'll hear a beautiful, heavenly sound coming down from the very throne of Almighty God! It's not the sound of God's anger! It's not the sound of God's wrath! It's the sound of the joy of the Lord, the sound of

HOLY LAUGHTER!

Holy Laughter